"Come here."

Austin reached down, grabbed her hand and drew Brooke to her feet. He put his hands on her face, cupping her cheeks in his palms.

"No one," he said firmly. "No one makes me do something I don't want to do. I'm not marrying you because I have to. I don't feel trapped. You're not taking advantage of my good nature."

Her eyes widened. "I'm not?"

He dragged her against him. "This marriage is convenient for me, too," he drawled. "I want you in my bed every night. I want you in a million different ways. I want to take you over and over again and make you cry out my name until neither of us can remember to breathe. You're a fire in my blood."

* * *

Million Dollar Baby is part of the Texas Cattleman's Club: Bachelor Auction series.

Dear Reader,

My husband and I met in high school and married between our sophomore and junior years in college. (FYI: we graduated together *and* on time—go us!) I barely remember *not* loving Charlie, so my firsthand knowledge of "dating" as a twentysomething adult is nonexistent.

When I am writing a book, I have to put myself in the shoes of many different characters whose life experiences are different from mine. In the case of Austin and Brooke, who meet in a Texas bar, it was really a leap of faith for me to imagine that scenario.

Not only that, but I had to empathize with what it would be like to grow up in a town where everybody knows your business (and knows your parents).

I had such fun writing this book. Brooke became very special to me as she struggled to have the life she wanted. And my heart ached for Austin, who felt things so deeply and yet was a loner in many ways.

Thanks for loving books!

Janice Maynard

JANICE MAYNARD

MILLION DOLLAR BABY

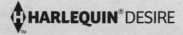

Special thanks and acknowledgment are given to Janice Maynard for her contribution to the Texas Cattleman's Club: Bachelor Auction miniseries.

Recycling programs for this product may not exist in your area.

ISBN-13: 978-1-335-97184-5

Million Dollar Baby

Copyright © 2018 by Harlequin Books S.A.

Printed in U.S.A.

www.Harlequin.com

USA TODAY bestselling author **Janice Maynard** loved books and writing even as a child. After multiple rejections, she finally sold her first manuscript! Since then, she has written fifty-plus books and novellas. Janice lives in Tennessee with her husband, Charles. They love hiking, traveling and family time. You can connect with Janice at www.janicemaynard.com, www.Twitter.com/janicemaynard, www.Facebook.com/janicemaynardreaderpage, www.Facebook.com/janicesmaynard and www.Instagram.com/janicemaynard.

Books by Janice Maynard

Harlequin Desire

The Kavanaghs of Silver Glen

A Not-So-Innocent Seduction
Baby for Keeps
Christmas in the Billionaire's Bed
Twins on the Way
Second Chance with the Billionaire
How to Sleep with the Boss
For Baby's Sake

Highland Heroes

His Heir, Her Secret
On Temporary Terms

Visit her Author Profile page at Harlequin.com, or janicemaynard.com, for more titles.

For the artists and dreamers among us...
May you always find ways to keep your
creative spirit alive. The world needs you!

* * *

Don't miss a single book in the
Texas Cattleman's Club: Bachelor Auction
series!

One

A dimly lit bar filled with rowdy patrons was an uncomfortable place to be on a Thursday night near the witching hour…if you were a woman without a date and too shy to make eye contact with anyone. The music was loud, masking Brooke's unease.

She was lonely and so very tired of being the forgotten Goodman child. She'd spent her entire life toeing some invisible line, and what had it gotten her? Neither of her parents respected her. Her two older brothers were out conquering the world. And where was Brooke? Stuck at home with Mom and Dad in Royal, Texas. Held hostage by their expectations and her own eager-to-please personality. The whole situation sucked.

She nursed her virgin strawberry daiquiri and stared at the tiny seeds nestling in the ice. Impulsive decisions were more her style than drunken peccadilloes. Brooke had seen too many of her friends almost ruin their lives with a single alcohol-fueled mistake. She might be crazy, but she was clearheaded.

Suddenly, she realized that the band had vacated the stage. The remaining plaintive music—courtesy of the lone guitar player—suited Brooke's mood. She didn't even mind the peanut-strewn floor and the smell of stale beer. At the same moment, she saw a man sitting alone at the bar, three empty stools on either side of him. Something about his broad shoulders made the breath catch in her throat. She had seen him walk in earlier. Instantaneous attraction might be a quirk of pheromones, but yearning had curled in the pit of her stomach even then. Sadly, the dance floor had been too crowded, and she had lost sight of him before she could work up the courage to introduce herself.

Now, here he was. All the scene needed was a shaft of light from heaven to tell her *this* was the man. *This* was her moment. She wanted him.

Butterflies fluttered through her. *Oh, God.* Was she really going to do it? Was she really going to pick up a stranger?

There was little question in her mind that he was her type. Even seated, she could tell that he was tall. His frame was leanly muscled and lanky, his posture relaxed. His dark blond hair—what she could see of it beneath the Stetson—was rumpled enough to be interesting and had a slight curl that gave him an approachable charm. Unfortunately, she couldn't gauge the color of his eyes from this distance.

Before she could change her mind, she lurched to her feet, frosty glass in hand, and made her way across the room. Not a single person stopped her. Not a single person joined the solitary man at the bar.

Surely it was a sign.

Taking a deep breath, she set her drink and her tiny clutch purse on the polished mahogany counter and hopped up on the leather-covered stool. No need to panic. It was only a conversation so far. That's all.

Now that she was close to him, she felt a little dizzy.

She gnawed her bottom lip and summoned a smile. "Hello, Cowboy. Mind if I join you?"

Austin glanced sideways and felt a kick of disappointment. The little blonde was a beauty, but she was far too young for him. Her gray eyes held an innocence he had lost years ago.

He shot her a terse smile. "Sorry, ma'am. I was about to leave."

Her face fell. "Oh, don't go. I thought we could chat."

He lifted an eyebrow. "Chat?"

Mortification stained her cheeks crimson. "Well, you know…"

"I *don't* know," he said. "That's the point. This could be a sorority prank, or maybe you're a not-quite-legal girl trying to lose her virginity. You look about sixteen, and I'm not keen to end up in jail tonight."

She scowled at him. "That's insulting."

"Not at all. You reek of innocence. It's a compliment, believe me. Unfortunately, I'm not the guy you're looking for."

"Maybe I want one who doesn't end sentences with prepositions."

The bite in her voice made him grin. "Are you insinuating that I'm uneducated?"

"Don't change the subject. For your information, I'm twenty-six. Plenty old enough to know my own mind." She took a deep breath. "I'm in the mood for romance."

"I think you mean sex."

He drawled the five words slowly, for nothing more than the pleasure of watching all that beautiful creamy skin turn a darker shade of dusky pink. "Sex?" The word came out as a tiny high-pitched syllable. Huge, smoky, thickly lashed eyes stared up at him.

This time he hid the grin. Poor kid was petrified.

He couldn't deny that he was tempted. She was genuine and sweet and disarmingly beautiful...in a healthy, girl-next-door kind of way. Her pale blond hair was caught up in a careless ponytail, and her royal-blue silk shirt and skinny jeans were nothing pretentious. Even her ballerina flats were unexceptional. She was the kind of woman who probably looked exactly this good when she rolled out of bed in the morning.

That thought took him down a road he needed to avoid. His sex hardened, making his pants uncomfortable. He held out his hand, attempting to normalize the situation. "I'm Au—"

She slapped her hand over his mouth, interrupting his polite introduction. "No," she said, sounding desperate and anxious all at the same time. "I'll call you Cowboy. You can call me Mandy."

He took her wrist and moved her hand away. "Not your real name?"

"No."

"Ah. Aliases. Intriguing."

"You're making fun of me." Her face fell.

"Maybe a little." He smiled to let her know he was teasing.

Without warning, their flirtatious repartee was rudely curtailed. A tall, statuesque redhead took the bar stool at his right shoulder and curled an arm around his waist. "Buy me another beer, will you? Sorry I was gone so long. Who the hell thinks it's a good idea to build a ladies' room with only a single stall?"

Austin groaned inwardly. *Damn.* He'd actually forgotten about Audra for a moment. "Um…"

Poor *Mandy* went dead white and looked as if she were going to throw up. "Excuse me," she said, with all the politeness of a guest at high tea with the queen. "It was a pleasure to meet you, but I have to go now."

Thank God Audra was a quick study. She sized up the situation in a glance. Her eyes widened. "Oh, crap. I'm sorry. Don't go. I'm his sister. Honest."

Mandy hesitated.

Austin nodded. "It's true. Underneath that bottled red hair is a blonde just like me."

Audra stood up and grimaced. "Forget the beer, little brother. I'll grab a cab. See you at the house later."

Then his five-years-older sister went completely off script. She stepped around him and took both of Mandy's hands in hers. "Here's the thing, ma'am. I know it's sometimes scary to meet men these days. Getting hit on in a bar can be dangerous."

"*She* was hitting on *me*," Austin muttered.

Both women ignored him.

Audra continued. "My brother is a good, decent man. He doesn't have any diseases, and he doesn't assault women. You don't have to be afraid of him."

"Audra!" His head threatened to explode from embarrassment.

Mandy barely glanced at him. "I see."

Audra nodded. "He doesn't live here. He's in town visiting me, and we came out tonight to…well…"

For once, his outrageous sister looked abashed.

Mandy gave him a puzzled look. "To what?"

Dear Lord. He gritted his teeth. If he didn't tell her, Audra would. "Today is the anniversary of my wife's death. She's been gone for six years. I finally took my wedding ring off, thanks to my sister's badgering. That's it. That's all."

Tears welled in Mandy's eyes. She blinked them back, but one rolled down her cheek. "I had no idea. I am so sorry."

Audra patted her shoulder. "It was a long time ago. He's fine."

Austin got to his feet and grabbed his sister's arm none too gently despite her glowing character testimonial. "You're leaving. Now."

He glanced back at Mandy. "Don't move."

On the way to the door, Audra smirked at him. "I won't wait up for you. Have fun tonight."

"You are such a brat."

Outside on the sidewalk, he hugged her. "I won't discuss my love life with you. A man has boundaries."

Audra kissed his cheek. "Understood. I just want you to be happy, that's all."

"I am happy," he said.

"Liar."

"I'm happier than I was."

"Go back in there before she gets cold feet."

"I love you, sis."

"I love you, too."

He watched his only sibling get into a cab, and then he looked through the window into the bar where not one but two men had taken advantage of his absence to move in on Mandy.

No way. No way in hell. The little blonde was his. At least for tonight.

Brooke breathed a sigh of relief when her cowboy returned and dispersed the crowd that had gathered around her. Apparently if the hour was late enough and the man drunk enough, even the most vehement no didn't register.

When it was just the two of them again, the cowboy gave her a slow, intimate smile that curled her toes. "May I buy you another drink?"

"No, thanks. I wasn't drinking. Not really. Alcohol clouds a person's judgment. I wanted to be clearheaded tonight."

"I see." He cocked his head and studied her. "Do you live here in Joplin?"

"Nope."

"So we're both just passing through?"

"It would seem that way."

A small grin teased the corners of his mouth. The man had a great mouth. Really great. She could imagine kissing that mouth all night long.

Finally, he shook his head, bemusement in his baffled gaze. "I know what *I'm* doing here, *Mandy*, but I'm still not clear about why you showed up at this bar tonight."

"Does it matter?" She hadn't expected a man to quiz her. The fact that her cowboy was slowing things down rattled her.

He nodded. "It does to me."

"Maybe I'm horny."

He snorted out a laugh and tried to turn it into a cough…unsuccessfully. Then he rubbed two fingers in the center of his forehead and sighed. "I'm not asking for your life story. But I'd like to know why me and why tonight. Is this a rebound thing? Are you trying to teach someone a lesson? Am I even warm?"

"Ninety-nine men out of a hundred would already have me in bed right now."

"Sorry to disappoint you."

The look in his eyes made her feel like a naughty schoolgirl. And not in a good way. She drained the last of her melted daiquiri and wrinkled her nose. "My life is boring. I'm having some family issues. For once I wanted to do something wild and exciting and totally out of character. Plus, you're really hot."

"So you *don't* frequent bars as a rule?"

"You know I don't," she grumbled, "or I wouldn't be so bad at it."

He flicked the end of her ponytail. "I never said you were bad at it."

Some deep note in his voice caught her stomach and sent it into a free fall of excitement and anticipation. "So are we good now?" she asked.

The cowboy stared at her. He stared at her for so long that her nipples pebbled and her thighs clenched. "What makes you believe that you and I will be wild and exciting? What if you chose wrong?"

She gaped. Words escaped her.

He closed her mouth with a finger below her chin. "It would seem prudent to take me out for a test drive ahead of time…don't you think?"

Before she could do more than inhale a sharp, startled breath, he slid one big hand beneath her ponytail, cupped the base of her neck and pulled her toward him just far enough for their mouths to meet comfortably.

Actually, *comfortable* was a misnomer for what happened next. Fireworks shot toward the ceiling in all directions. Angel choirs sang. A million dizzying pinwheels shot through her veins and rocketed into her pelvis.

The man was kissing her. Nothing more. So why was the earth shaking beneath her feet?

He tasted of whiskey and temptation. If she'd had any remaining reservations about her plan, they vanished in the heat of his lips on hers. It was possible she whimpered. She definitely leaned in and wordlessly begged for more.

Somewhere in the distance catcalls and whoops and hollers signaled an appreciative audience. But Brooke barely noticed. Her hands settled on the cowboy's shoulders. "Take off your hat," she begged.

"I only take off the hat in bed," he said, the words rough with lust and determination.

"Oh."

His smile was more of a grimace. "It's not too late for you to walk away. In fact, it's never too late. You started this little fantasy, but you can say no whenever you want."

She looked up at him, feeling the oddest combination of confidence and stomach-curling uncertainty. "I don't want to say no."

"Do you have a hotel room?"

"Not yet."

"Any preference?"

"Not somewhere fancy." Translation—nowhere that the staff might know her parents.

His terse nod seemed to indicate agreement. "Let's go, then." He tossed money on the bar for the tab and took her elbow as they walked out.

Outside, they paused on the sidewalk. It was August, and the air was pleasant at this hour. He pointed at a late-model pickup truck. "Would you like me to drive?"

Brooke shook her head. Who knew that the mechanics of a one-night stand were so tricky? "My things are in my car. I'll meet you there. How about the Sherwood Hotel? Two streets over?"

"I know it."

"I'm sorry," she said, feeling brutally young and stupid.

"For what?"

"I'm sorry you lost your wife."

He cursed beneath his breath, rolled his shoulders and stared up at the moon, his profile starkly masculine. "You told me we weren't going to use our real names," he said. "That was *your* rule. Well, mine is no rehashing the past. This is sex, Mandy. Wild and exciting and temporary—if that's not what you want, walk away."

His entire body vibrated with tension. She honestly couldn't tell if he was angry or sexually frustrated or both.

In that moment, she realized that her reasons for coming to Joplin no longer existed. She wasn't here to flirt or to pick up a stranger or to have an anonymous tryst to prove to herself that she wasn't boring.

Right here, right now…with her limbs shaking and her mouth dry and her nerves shot…the only thing she wanted was to undress this cowboy and to have him return the favor. Because this man, this beautiful, hauntingly complicated man, tugged at her heartstrings. She wanted to know him in every way there was to know a lover.

She only had one night. It would have to be enough.

Daringly, she reached out and put a hand on his arm. She could feel his taut, warm muscles through the soft cotton fabric of his shirt. "I don't want to walk away, Cowboy. I'll meet you at the hotel. Don't make me wait."

Two

Austin Bradshaw couldn't be entirely sure he wasn't dreaming. This night was like nothing he had ever experienced. He glanced in his rearview mirror to make sure Mandy's little navy Honda was still behind him. He chuckled to himself, because he had a hunch the car was a rental. His mystery woman struck him as the kind of person who would attend to the details of a plan with great care.

The desk clerk at the midrange hotel was neither curious nor particularly friendly. He swiped Austin's credit card, handed over two keys and immediately returned his focus to whatever show he was watching on his laptop.

When Austin went back outside, he found Mandy leaning against the side of his pickup, an overnight case in her hand. She shifted from one foot to the other. "All set?"

He stared at her. "Are you sure you want to do this?"

"Quit asking me that," she huffed. "I'm here, aren't I?"

Releasing a slow, steady breath, he took the bag out of her death grip and set it on the ground. Then he cupped her head in his hands, tilted her face up to his and crushed his mouth over hers. He'd been in a state of arousal now for the better part of two hours. The faint scent of her perfume and the taste of her lips were imprinted on his brain.

He wanted her. Naked. Hungry. Begging. The more he thought about the night to come, the more he unraveled. At the rate they were going, there wasn't going to be much of the night left.

Reluctantly, he let her go. "Hurry," he said.

The hotel was three stories tall with indoor corridors and modern decor. At this point, Austin could have taken her up against the wall in the stairwell, but he resisted.

They rode the elevator to the top floor. Their room was at the end on the corner. His hand shook so badly it took him three tries to get the key in the door. He expected Mandy to give him grief about it, but she never said a word.

When they were finally inside, he closed the door carefully in deference to their fellow guests and leaned against it.

Mandy frowned. "Where's your bag?"

"I don't have one."

"Why not?"

"That's not really how a one-night stand works, honey."

She looked mortified. "Why didn't you tell me?"

"I thought you'd be more comfortable if you had your bag. Women like to have their little bits and pieces with them."

Mandy wrapped her arms around her waist and scanned the room like she was casing it for fire exits.

"What's wrong?" he asked, reminding himself that patience was a virtue.

Her bottom lip trembled. "I just realized something. If tonight is your first time to have sex in six years, I can't go through with this. That's too much pressure for me. Honestly."

He burst out laughing, and then laughed even harder at the look of indignation on her face. "Not to worry," he said, wiping his cheeks and trying to get himself under control. His companion clearly didn't see the humor in the situation. "I've had sex. Occasionally. And besides, if what you said were true, we'd never have made it out of the parking lot back at the bar. So no pressure, okay? Just you and me and all that wild excitement you wanted."

Some of the tension drained from her body. "Oh. Well, that's good. I guess."

"Come here, honey." He held out his hand.

She came to him willingly. But her gaze didn't quite meet his, and her cheeks were flushed.

He unbuttoned the top button of her shirt. "Your skin is like cream. Beautiful and smooth." Brushing the tops of her breasts with his fingertips, he smiled inwardly when she sighed.

"You're still wearing your hat," she said.

"And we're still not in bed."

"Close enough." She reached up and took off his Stetson. After tossing it on the nearest chair, she massaged his head with both hands. "You shouldn't cover up your hair. Women would kill for this color."

He could tell she was more comfortable with him now. That was a very good thing, because he didn't want a timid partner in bed. "Feel free to take off anything else that catches your fancy."

"Very funny." She toyed with his belt buckle. "Why aren't you calling me Mandy?"

"Because you don't look like a Mandy. It's not your real name. So I'll stick with *honey*. Unless you want to fess up and tell me the truth. It's not like I'm going to stalk you."

"I know that." The snippy response was the tiniest bit sulky. And her bottom lip stuck out. It was so damned cute, he wanted to suck on it.

Gently, he pulled her shirt loose from the waistband of her jeans and slid his hands underneath. Her skin was warm and soft. So soft. He wanted to make this night good for her.

He unhooked her bra. It still bothered him that he didn't know why she was here…not really. But his brain was losing the battle with the driving urge to give her what she wanted. What *he* wanted.

When he slipped her shirt from her shoulders and took her bra right along with it, she didn't protest. The sight of her standing there, all white creamy skin and big gray eyes and rosy pink nipples, stole his breath and tightened his gut. "God, you're gorgeous," he said huskily, breathing it like a prayer.

He hadn't lied to her. There had been a handful of women in six years. But those had been *real* one-night stands. Women whose names and faces he barely remembered. Divorcées. Widows hurting like he was. The sex had slaked a momentary physical need, but afterward, his grief had been just as deep, just as raw.

In a way, it had been easier *not* to have sex, because that way he didn't have to be reminded of all he had lost.

He scooped her up in his arms and carried her to the bed. Something about tonight felt different. Maybe because his mystery woman was ridiculously charming and vulnerable and maybe even a little bit naive. She brought out his protective instincts and tapped into raw emotions inside him that he would have sworn were dead and buried.

With her he felt the need to be tender.

"Hang on, honey." Hitching her higher on his chest, he grabbed for the comforter with one hand and dragged it and the sheet halfway down the bed. Then he dropped the big-eyed blonde on the mattress and tried not to pounce on her. Instead, he came down beside her and propped his head on his hand.

Lazily, he traced a fingertip from her collarbone, down between her breasts, over her concave belly to her tiny cute navel. "Tell me what you're thinking, sweet lady. I swear I don't bite."

Her body was so rigid it was giving *him* a headache.

She gnawed her lower lip. "I forgot about protection."

"Not to worry. We're good for two rounds." He reached in his back pocket and extracted a duo of condom packets. "I had these in the truck."

"Oh. That's nice."

"Tell me your name," he coaxed. He bent over her and kissed his way from her navel up along her rib cage, pausing just at the slope of her breast and waiting until her breathing ratcheted up a notch and a shudder worked its way through her body.

"You're not playing fair…" She gazed up at him from underneath sultry lashes.

Did she have any idea what that look did to a man? He flicked his tongue across her nipple…barely a graze. "I play to win, honey. You wanted wild and exciting? That usually means breaking the rules."

He was breathing hard, barely holding it together. Playing this game was fun, more fun than he'd had in a hell of a long time. But he wasn't sure how much longer he could last. Already he wanted her so badly he was shaking.

"Brooke," she whispered. "My name is Brooke."

The trust on her face made him ashamed. She was doing something out of character. He knew it. And he was prepared to help her in her quest for a night of reckless passion. What kind of man did that make him?

He swallowed hard. "Brooke. I like it. With an *e* or no *e*?"

She smiled. "Does it matter?"

"It does to me." And it did. When this was over and they went their separate ways, he wanted to remember her exactly like this. He wanted to know everything there was to know.

She caressed his chin, feeling the stubble. He'd shaved at six that morning. "With an *e*, Cowboy. Now it's your turn."

He didn't pretend to misunderstand. "Austin," he groaned. "My name is Austin." Moving his lips across her breast, he kissed his way up hills and down valleys and back again until Brooke panted and whimpered and begged. That was the sign he had been waiting for.

He rolled to his feet and ripped at his shirt, dragging it over his head in one frustrated motion. Then he toed off his boots and shucked out of his jeans and boxers. When he was buck-ass naked, he stood beside the bed and tried to catch his breath. It was embarrassing to be so winded when he hadn't even started yet.

Brooke came up on her knees and stared. "Are you normal?"

He blinked. "Excuse me?"

She waved a hand. "Your, um…you know. It seems kind of big."

A slither of unease sent ice water through his veins. "You wouldn't lie to me about that virgin thing. Would you?"

She straightened her shoulders, her eyes flashing. "I am *not* a liar."

"So you've definitely had sex."

"Of course."

"How many times?"

"That's none of your business." She unbuttoned her jeans and shimmied them down her thighs.

His mouth went dry. "I was gonna do that."

She gave him a look. "You were taking too long. I'm not sure I picked the right man. Are you positive you know what you're doing?"

He didn't know whether to laugh or howl with frustration. "God, you're a piece of work."

"You promised me wild and exciting. I'm still wearing panties."

He grabbed her around the waist and tumbled them both to the bed, rolling so they landed with Brooke on top. She was easily eight inches shorter than he was and forty pounds lighter. She pretended to struggle. He pretended to let her. When they were both breathless, he kissed her hard.

She melted into him, purring his name with soft, erotic yearning that made every cell in his body ache.

He rubbed her back. "I'm glad you walked into my life tonight, Brooke with no last name." Her ponytail had come loose. Pale, sunshiny hair tumbled around them, soft and silky. It smelled like lilacs and innocence and happy summer afternoons.

She nibbled his chin. "Me, too. I nearly chickened out, but then I saw you sitting there, and I felt something."

"Something?" He palmed her bottom. It was a perfect bottom. Plump and pert and exactly the right size for a man's hands.

"A zing, I guess. Animal attraction." She shifted her weight and nearly injured him. He was so hard his balls ached. The condom was in arm's reach. All he had to do was grab it. But he didn't want this to be over. He didn't want the night to end.

Without warning, Brooke rolled off him, settled onto her side, and took his sex in her hand. "I like the way you look, Cowboy." She stroked him slowly, her gaze focused on the task at hand.

The feel of her cool slender fingers on his taut flesh skated the line between pleasure and pain. He gritted his teeth and tried not to come. "I told you my name," he groaned.

She rested her cheek on his shoulder and continued her torture. "Yes, you did." She gripped him tightly. "Austin." She whispered it low and sweet.

Sweat broke out on his brow. This woman was killing him slowly...

Brooke was hot and dizzy and elated. For an idea that had begun so badly, this was turning out to be a night to remember. Austin was everything she could have asked for in a lover. Demanding and yet tender. Tough and masculine, but still considerate of her insecurities.

He grabbed her wrist and moved it away from his erection. "Enough," he croaked.

Before she could protest, he reached for the condom, rolled it on and dragged her panties down her legs. Then he was on top of her and in her and she forgot how to breathe.

He was heavy and wildly aroused. Thankfully, she was equally excited. Despite his impressive stats, her body accepted him easily. It had been a long time for her, but he didn't have to know that. She canted her hips, tried to relax and concentrated on the incredible sensation of fullness as her body became one with his.

Something about the moment dampened her eyes and tightened her throat. Maybe it was the thought of all he had lost. Maybe it was a breathless yearning to have a man like this for her own one day. Whatever it was, it made her weepy and left her feeling raw and vulnerable. As if it were impossible to hide from him.

He came quickly, with a muttered apology, his chest heaving. Brooke tried to squelch her disappointment. After a quick trip to the bathroom to dispose of the condom, he returned. In their hurry, they had left the lamp on. Now, he flipped the switch, plunging the room into darkness. Only an automatic night-light in the bathroom dispersed some of the gloom as their eyes adjusted.

Austin smoothed the hair from her face. "I'm sorry about that, honey. You had me pretty wound up, and it's been a little while for me."

"It's fine."

His grin was a flash of white. "It's *not* fine. But it will be. Spread your legs, darlin'. Let me show you the fireworks."

She moved her ankles apart obediently, but inside, she grimaced. This had never been her strong suit. It was too personal, too intimate. The only man who had ever gotten this far with her had been really bad at it.

Fortunately, Austin wasn't privy to her negative thoughts. He cradled her head in his arm and touched her with confidence, the confidence of a man who knew how to pleasure a woman and liked doing it. "Close your eyes," he crooned. "Relax, Brooke."

It was only when he said those two words that she realized her fingers were clenched in the sheets and her shoulders were rigid. "Sorry," she muttered. "You don't have to do this."

Austin frowned. "I need to touch you. Your body is beautiful and soft and so damn sexy. I want to hear you scream my name."

"Arrogant cowboy…"

He entered her with two fingers and used his thumb to stroke the spot where she ached the most. The keening cry that escaped her throat was embarrassing. But soon, embarrassment was the furthest thing from her mind.

Austin decimated her. He whispered naughty things and caressed her with sure steady touches until her own responses shocked her and her body became a stranger. Just as her spine arched off the bed, she did indeed scream his name. Moments later, he moved on top of her and entered her a second time.

The orgasm was incredible. On a scale of one to ten, it was some imaginary number that only scientists from outer space could decipher.

This time, Austin was just getting started as she tumbled down the far side of the hill. He laughed roughly and shoved her up the peak again, thrusting harder and faster and holding her tightly until they both found the pinnacle at almost the same moment and lost themselves in the fiery pleasure.

Brooke was boneless, elated and utterly spent. Never again would she settle for the kind of relationship that was boring and mundane. This wonderful cowboy had given her that.

They lay together in a tangle of arms and legs as their bodies cooled and their heartbeats slowed.

At last, Austin shifted so she wasn't bearing his full weight. "You okay?" he asked, sounding sleepy and sated and maybe a little bit smug.

She nuzzled her head against his warm, hard shoulder. "Oh, yeah. Better than okay." Tomorrow morning, she was going to get online and give this hotel five stars across the board.

He groaned and rolled away. "Don't move. I'm coming back."

She heard the water run in the bathroom. Then silence. Then a low curse.

"What's wrong?" she said, raising her voice in alarm.

He stumbled back into bed, his skin chilled. "The condom broke." His voice was flat. She couldn't read him at all.

"Oh."

"I'm sorry."

"It's okay. I'm on the pill. For other reasons. And besides, it's the wrong time of the month." She was due to start her period any day, actually.

"I'm healthy, Brooke. Nothing to worry about there."

"Then we're in the clear."

He yawned and pulled her into his arms, spooning her from behind. "Let me sleep for an hour, and we can go again."

"You're out of condoms."

He kissed the nape of her neck. "We'll improvise."

Brooke lay perfectly still and felt the exact moment when Austin crashed hard. His breathing deepened. The arm that encircled her became heavy.

She knew the time had come for her to go home, but she couldn't leave him. Not yet. This night had turned into something she hadn't anticipated, something she hadn't really wanted.

Here was a man who had known pain and loss. Even if they lived in the same town, he wouldn't want a woman like her. She couldn't even stand up to her parents. She had her own battles to fight. And she would have to do it without this sweet, gruff cowboy.

She inhaled his scent. Tried to memorize it. The way his body held hers seemed fated somehow. But that was a lie. He was a man she had picked up in a bar. A man with demons, like any other man.

Carefully, with her chest tight and her hands shaking, she extracted herself from his arms one heartbeat at a time. It wasn't easy. Fortunately, Austin slept like the dead. Once she was out of the bed, the rest went smoothly.

She visited the bathroom. She dressed quietly. She took her bag and her purse and slipped out into the hall.

On the other side of the door, she started to shake. Leaving her one-night stand cowboy was the hardest thing she had ever had to do.

The drive from Joplin to Royal in the middle of the night seemed surreal. Punching in the alarm code and sneaking into the house was almost anticlimactic. She was too tired to shower. Instead, she tumbled into bed and fell asleep instantly.

Three

Two months later

Austin parked his truck across the street from the Texas Cattleman's Club, got out and stretched. It had been three years...maybe four...since he had last been in Royal, Texas. Not much had changed. An F4 tornado a while back had destroyed a few homes and businesses and damaged others, but the town had rebuilt.

The club itself was a historic structure over a hundred years old. The rambling single-story building with its dark stone-and-wood exterior and tall slate roof was an icon in the area. Ordinarily, Austin wouldn't be the kind of guy to darken the doors, but he was meeting Gus Slade here at 10:00 a.m.

Austin had plenty of money in the bank...likely more than he would ever need. But he didn't have the blue-blooded ranching pedigree that men like Gus respected. Still, Gus had invited him here to do a job, and Austin had agreed.

Audra was right. He'd been drifting since Jenny died. It was time to get his business back on track. He'd rambled all over a five-county area in recent years doing odd jobs to pay the bills. The truth was, he was a damned good architect and had been wasting his skills.

Even this job with Gus was a throwaway. But it could open the doors to something more significant, so he had jumped at the chance.

He took his time crossing the street. No need to look too eager. Already, he had made concessions. Instead of his usual jeans and flannel shirt, he had worn neatly pressed khakis, a spotless white dress shirt with the sleeves rolled up and his best pair of boots. Cowboys came in all shapes and sizes in Texas. Austin was shooting for ambitious professional for today's meeting.

It was who he had been once upon a time. Until Jenny got sick...

Shoving away the unhappy memories, he ran a hand through his hair, flipped his phone to silent mode and strode through the imposing front doors. A smiling receptionist directed him to one of the private meeting rooms partway down the hall.

Augustus "Gus" Slade was already there, deep in conversation with two other men. When Austin appeared, Gus's two companions said their goodbyes and exited.

Gus held out his hand. "There you are, boy. Right on the money. Thanks for coming. It's been a long time."

"It's good to see you, sir. Thanks for offering me the job."

Gus was an imposing figure of a man. He was tall and solidly built with a full head of snow-white hair. Piercing eyes that were blue like the Texas sky reflected a keen intelligence.

By Austin's calculations, the man was probably sixty-eight or sixty-nine. He could have passed for a decade younger were it not for the leatherlike quality of his skin. He'd spent decades working in the sun long before warnings about skin cancer were the norm.

At a time in life when many men his age began to think about traveling or playing golf or simply taking things easy, Gus still worked his cattle ranch, the Lone Wolf, and wielded his influence in Royal. He had plenty of the latter to go around and had even served a few terms as TCC president. Though the burly rancher loved his family and was well respected by the community at large, most people knew he could be fierce when crossed or angered.

Austin had no plans to do either.

At Gus's urging, Austin settled into one of a pair of wing-backed chairs situated in front of a large fireplace. The weather in Royal was notably mercurial. Yesterday, it had been in the fifties and raining. Today, the temperature was pushing seventy, and the skies were sunny, so no fire.

Gus took the second chair with a grimace and rubbed

his knee. "Got kicked by a damned bull. Should have known better."

Austin nodded and smiled. "I worked cattle during the summers when I was in college. It was a great job, but I went to bed sore many a night." He hesitated half a breath and plunged on. "So tell me about this job you want me to do."

When he had been in Royal before, Gus had wanted him to design and build an addition onto his home. Austin had still been paying for Jenny's medical bills, and he had needed the money. So he had worked his ass off for six months...or maybe it was seven.

He'd been proud of the job, and Gus had been pleased.

The older man twisted his mouth into a slight grimace. "I may have brought you here under false pretenses. It's not like last time. This will be a one-and-done project. But as I mentioned on the phone, I think being here at the club for a few weeks will give you the chance to meet some folks in Royal who are movers and shakers. These are the kind of men and women who have contacts. They know people and can make things happen to push work your way."

Austin wasn't sure how he felt about that. On the one hand, it made sense to rebuild his career. It had stalled out when he made the choice to stay home with Jenny during what turned out to be the last months of her life. It was a choice he had never regretted.

Even in the depths of his grief, when he had drifted from town to town and job to job, his skill set and work ethic had made it possible for him to command significant compensation for his quality work.

Did he really want to go back to a more structured way of life?

He honestly didn't know.

And because he didn't, he equivocated. "I appreciate that, sir. But how about you tell me the details of this particular project?"

"The club is hoping to do more with the outside space than we have in the past. Professional landscapers are in the process of developing a site plan for the area around the gardens and the pool. What I want from you is a permanent outdoor venue that will serve as the stage for the charity auction and can later be used for weddings, etc. The audience, or the guests, will be out front…under a circus tent if the weather demands it."

"So open air, but covered."

"You got it. Plus, we want the stage to have at least two or three rooms behind the scenes with bathrooms and changing areas…you get the idea."

"And what is this auction exactly?"

Gus chuckled. "It's a mouthful…the Great Royal Bachelor Auction." He sobered. "To benefit the Pancreatic Cancer Foundation. That's what my Sarah died of, you know. My granddaughter Alexis is on the foundation board. I'd like for you to meet her. Your wife has been gone a long time. It's not good for a man to be alone."

"I mean no disrespect, sir, but you don't seem to be taking your own advice. And beyond that, I have no interest at all in a relationship, though I'm sure your granddaughter is delightful."

Gus scowled at him. "Maybe you shouldn't be so quick to turn her down. A lot of men would jump at the chance to have my blessing."

Austin smiled. "If Alexis is anything like her grandfather, I'm guessing she doesn't appreciate you meddling in her affairs."

"That's true enough," Gus said. "She seems determined to fritter away her time with a man who is all wrong for her."

They had strayed off topic again, which made Austin realize that Gus was inordinately interested in matchmaking. He sighed. "I'll need a budget. And the exact specs of the area where I'm allowed to build."

"Money's no object," the older man said. "We want top-of-the-line all the way. And make sure to include some kind of outdoor heating units, concealed if possible. You know how it is in Texas. We might wear shorts on Christmas Day, and it can snow eight hours later."

"What's my timetable?" Austin asked.

"The auction is the last Saturday in November."

Austin tried to conceal his shock. "Cutting it a little close, aren't you?"

Gus nodded. "I know. It will be tight. But the club's custodial staff has been given instructions to help you in any way possible, and we've also allotted extra funds to hire part-time carpenters to rough in the framing and anything else you need. I have faith in you, boy."

"Thank you, sir. I won't let you down."

"Call me Gus. I insist."

After that, they made their way outside so Austin could see exactly what he had to work with. Despite his reservations about the quick turnaround, excitement bubbled up in his chest. This was always one of his favorite phases of a project—looking at a bare plot of ground and imagining the possibilities.

The gardens were soggy, but Austin could see that someone had already begun placing markers and lining off planting areas.

Gus pointed. "Over there is where the stage will be."

Austin nodded. "I can work with that."

In the distance, he could see the pool, now closed for the season. The new structure would tie in with the gardens and the rear of the original building to create a peaceful, idyllic setting for entertaining.

To their left, a small figure in stained overalls stood three feet off the ground on a stepladder painting a colorful mural on an outer wall of the club. Gus waved a hand. "Let's go say hello," he said.

It was only a matter of fifteen yards. Twenty at the most. They were close enough for Austin to recognize the pale, silky ponytail when it hit him.

The woman turned around as Gus hailed her. The paintbrush in her hand clattered to the ground. Her face turned white. She clutched the top of the ladder.

Austin sucked in a shocked breath. It was *her*. Brooke. His mystery lover.

Only a clueless fool would have missed the tension, and Gus was no fool. He frowned. "Do you two know each other?"

Austin waited. Ladies first. Brooke stared at him,

her eyes curiously blank. "Not at all," she said politely. "How do you do? I'm Brooke Goodman."

What the hell? Austin had no choice but to follow her lead. Or else call her a liar. He stuck out his hand. "Austin Bradshaw. Nice to meet you."

The air crackled with electricity. Brooke didn't take his hand. She held up both of hers, palms out, to show they were paint streaked. "You'll have to excuse me. I don't want to get you dirty." She shifted her attention to Gus. "If you two don't mind, I'm trying to get this section finished quickly. They tell me another band of showers is going to move in tonight, so the paint needs to dry."

And just like that, she turned her back and shut him out.

Four

Brooke felt so ill she was afraid she might pass out right there on the ladder. She stood perfectly still and pretended to paint the same four-inch square of wall until she heard a door open and shut. Out of the corner of her eye she saw the two men disappear inside the building.

What was Austin doing in Royal? Had he come to find her? Surely not. He'd been with Gus Slade. If she put two and two together, maybe Austin was the architect Gus had hired to build the fancy stage and outdoor annex. How did Gus even know Austin?

Who could she ask? Alexis? Then again, did she really want to draw attention to the fact that she was interested in Austin? She wasn't. Not at all.

Liar.

What made the situation even worse was the expression on Austin's face when he saw her. He'd been equal parts flabbergasted and horrified. Not the look a woman wanted to see from a man she'd spent the night with.

And see what he'd done to her, damn it…now he had *her* ending sentences with prepositions.

When the coast was clear, she wiped her brush and gathered her supplies. Ordinarily, she went inside the club to a utility sink and cleaned up before going home. Today, she couldn't take that chance.

For the rest of the afternoon and all night long, she fretted. She'd spent the last eight weeks trying to forget about her one-night-stand cowboy. Now he had appeared in Royal, completely out of the blue, and looking about ten times as gorgeous and sexy as she remembered. If he really was the new architect, she was going to be forced to see him repeatedly.

Her body thought that was a darned good idea. Heat sizzled through her veins. But her brain was smarter and more sensible. This was a bad development. Really bad.

The following morning, when the sun came up on another beautiful October day, she wanted to pull the covers over her head and not have to *think*. Still, the memories came rushing back. An intimate hotel room. A rugged cowboy. Two naked bodies. What was she going to do? With yummy Austin in town, there would be hell to pay if her secret came out.

More than ever, she needed to get her own place to live. With the money Alexis was paying her for the murals, there would soon be enough in her modest bank account for first and last month's rent on a decent apartment. In three and a half years, she would receive her inheritance from her grandmother and thus be able to start her after-school art program. Everybody took dance lessons and played sports—Brooke wanted to build a small studio where dreamy kids like she had been could dabble in clay and paint to their heart's content.

All she had to do in the meantime was find a permanent job, any job, that would give her financial independence from her parents. That task was tough in a town where the Goodmans pulled strings right and left. Brooke had been unofficially blacklisted time and again.

Her parents' behind-the-scenes manipulations were humiliating and infuriating. And all because they wanted her to be the kind of high-powered entrepreneurs they were.

It was never going to happen. Brooke liked who she was. It wasn't that she lacked ambition. She simply saw a different path for herself.

Fortunately, her parents were both early risers and left for the office at the crack of dawn. Brooke was able to enjoy her toast and coffee in peace. Her stomach rebelled at the thought of food this morning, probably because she was so upset about the prospect of seeing Austin again.

What was she supposed to say to him?

Could she simply avoid him altogether?

She was small. Maybe she could hide.

When she couldn't put it off any longer, she drove into town. Her parents' Pine Valley mansion had been her childhood home. She'd left it only to go to college and grad school. Now it had become a prison. Her whole family was seriously broken in her estimation. Her brother Jared's poor fiancée had been forced to run away from her own wedding to escape.

Brooke was still trying to find a way out. It wasn't as easy as it sounded. But she was at least working on a plan.

When she arrived at the club, she parked one street over and gathered up the canvas totes that contained her supplies. At least she knew what Austin's truck looked like. So far, she didn't see it anywhere around. Maybe he was at his hotel doing whatever architects did on their laptops before they started a new job.

Hopefully she could get her murals done before he showed up again. Didn't a project like this require site prep? Surely an architect wasn't involved in that phase.

Her heart slugged in her chest. This was exactly why she had gone to another town for her secret fling. She hadn't wanted to face any ramifications of her indiscretion afterward.

Remembering that night was both mortifying and deeply arousing. What thoughts had gone through his head when he woke up and found her missing? She had second-guessed that decision a thousand times.

In the end, though, it had been the only choice. She and Austin had been strangers passing in the night. Joplin wasn't home for either of them. It had been the perfect anonymous scenario.

Except now it wasn't.

To access the gardens, it was first necessary to go through the club. She greeted the receptionist and made her way down the corridor hung with hunting trophies and artifacts. Both of her parents had been members here for years. The building was familiar.

What wasn't so familiar was the sensation of apprehension and excitement. She told herself she didn't want to see Austin Bradshaw again. But the lie wasn't very believable, even in her head.

It was almost anticlimactic to arrive in the gardens and find herself completely alone. The landscaping crew came and went at odd hours. This morning, no one was around to disturb Brooke's concentration. Up until now, she had enjoyed the time to focus on her creations, to dream and to let her imagination run wild. Today, the solitude felt disconcerting.

Doggedly, she uncapped her paints and planned the section she would work on next. It was a large-scale, multilevel task. Instead of two long gray stucco walls at right angles to one another, Alexis had charged Brooke with creating a whimsical extension of the gardens. When spring came and the flowers bloomed, there would be no delineation between the actual gardens and Brooke's fantasy world.

The work challenged her creativity and her vision. Not only did she have to paint on a very large canvas, but she had to think in bold, thematic strokes. It was the most ambitious project she had ever tackled, and she was honored that Alexis trusted her to handle the makeover.

When the stage was built, the new landscaping was complete and Brooke's paintings were finished, the outdoor area would be spectacular. It felt good to be part of something that would provide enjoyment to so many people.

She selected the appropriate brush and tucked it behind her ear. Soon she would need a taller ladder, but for now, she was going to finish the portion she had abandoned yesterday. It was a border of daisies and baby rabbits that repeated along one edge of her mural.

Grabbing the metal frame that held four small paint pots, she climbed up three steps and cocked her head. White first. Then the yellow centers.

"Are you avoiding me, Brooke?"

The voice startled her so badly she flung paint all over herself and a huge section of blank wall and the grass below. "Austin," she cried.

He took her by the waist, lifted her and set her on the ground. "So you *do* know who I am." He smirked. "Yesterday, I wasn't so sure."

She scowled at him, trying not to notice the way sunlight picked out strands of gold in his hair without his hat. "What was I supposed to do? I couldn't tell Gus how we met."

Austin's lips quirked in the kind of superior male smile that made her want to smack him. "Most people would have come up with a polite lie."

"I'm a terrible liar," she said.

"I'll have to remember that. It might come in handy."

The intimate light in his warm brown eyes and the way he looked at her as if he were remembering every nanosecond of their night together made heat curl in her sex. "Why are you here, Austin?"

"I have a job to do. Why are *you* here, Brooke Goodman?"

"I live in Royal. And I have a job to do as well. So that makes this terribly awkward."

"Not at all." He eyed her mural. "This is your work? It's fabulous. You're very talented."

His praise warmed her. Other than Alexis, few people knew what she was capable of doing—at least, few people in Royal. "Thank you," she said. "I still have a long way to go."

"Which means I'll get to watch as I build the stage."

Her heart stuttered. He didn't mean anything by that statement...did he? "Austin, I—"

He held up his hand. "You don't have to say a word. I can see it on your face. You're afraid I'll spill your secret. But I won't, Brooke, I swear. You had your reasons for what happened in Joplin, and so did I." He cleared his throat, then went on. "The truth is, as much as I like you, we need to leave the past in the past. I'm done with relationships, trust me. And in a town like this, you clearly can't do anything without the whole world knowing your business."

He was saying all the right things. Exactly what she needed to hear.

So why did she have a knot in her stomach?

"I should get started," she said.

"For the record, I was damned disappointed when I woke up and you were gone."

"You were?" She searched his face.

He nodded slowly. "Yes."

"It was an amazing night for me, but I didn't have much basis for comparison."

He chuckled. "Your instincts were spot-on. If I were in the market for a girlfriend and you were five years older, we might give it a go."

Her temper flared. "Do you have any idea how arrogant you sound? I'm getting very tired of everybody in my life thinking they know what's best for me."

"Define *everybody*."

Brooke looked over his shoulder and grimaced. "Here comes one now."

Margaret Goodman was dressed impeccably from head to toe. Though she was well into her fifties, she could easily pass for a much younger woman. Her blond hair, sprinkled with only the slightest gray, received the attention of an expensive stylist every three weeks, and she had both a personal trainer and a dietitian on her payroll.

Brooke's mother was ambitious, driven and ice-cold. She was also—at the moment—clearly furious. A tiny splotch of red on each cheekbone betrayed her agitation.

"What are you doing here, Mama?" Brooke stepped forward, away from the cowboy architect, hoping to defuse the situation and at the same time possibly avoid any interaction between her mother and Austin.

Her mother lifted her chin. "Are you trying to spite me on purpose? Do you have any idea how humiliating it is to know that my only daughter is grubbing around in the gardens of the Texas Cattleman's Club like a common laborer?"

Brooke straightened her backbone. "Alexis Slade hired me to do a job. That's what I'm doing."

"Don't be naive and ridiculous. This isn't a job." Her mother flung a hand toward the partially painted wall in a dramatic gesture. "A child could do this. You're avoiding your potential, Brooke. Your father and I won't have it. It was bad enough that you changed your major in college without telling us. We paid for you to get a serious education, not a worthless art degree. Goodmans are businesspeople, Brooke. We *make* money, we don't squander it. When will you realize that playing with paint isn't a valid life choice?"

Her mother was shouting now, her disdain and reproach both vicious and hurtful.

Brooke had heard it all before, but with Austin as a witness, it was even more upsetting. Her eyes stung. "This *is* a real job, Mama. I'm proud of the work I'm doing. And for the record, I'm planning on moving out of the house, so you and Daddy might as well get used to the idea."

"Don't you speak to me in that tone."

"You don't listen any other way. I'm twenty-six years old. The boys moved out when they were twenty-one."

"Don't bring your brothers into this. They were both far more mature than you at this age. Neither of them gave us any grief."

Brooke shook her head, incredulous. Her brothers were sycophants and weasels who coasted by on their family connections and their willingness to suck up to Mommy and Daddy. "I won't discuss this with you right now. You're embarrassing me."

For the first time, Margaret looked at Austin. "Who is this?" she demanded, her nose twitching as if sniffing out an impostor in her blue-blooded world.

Before Brooke could stop him, Austin stepped forward, hand outstretched. "I'm Austin Bradshaw, ma'am…the architect Gus Slade hired to build the stage addition for the bachelor auction. I'm pleased to meet you."

His sun-kissed good looks and blinding smile caught Margaret midtirade. Her mouth opened and shut. "Um…"

Brooke sensed trouble brewing. She took her mother's arm and tried to steer her toward the building. "You don't want to get paint on your clothes, Mama, and I really need to get back to work. We'll discuss this tonight."

Margaret bristled. "I'm not finished talking to you, young lady. Put this mess away and come home."

"I won't," Brooke said. She felt ill, but she couldn't let her dislike of confrontation or the fact that they had an audience allow her mother to steamroll her. "I've made a commitment, and I intend to honor it."

Margaret scowled. When Brooke's mother was on a rant, people scattered. She could be terrifying. "I demand that you come with me this instant."

Brooke swallowed hard as bile rose in her throat. She wasn't wearing a hat, so the sun beat down on her head. Little yellow spots danced in front of her eyes, and her knees wobbled.

This was a nightmare.

But then, to her complete and utter shock, Austin intervened. He literally inserted himself between Brooke and her mother, shielding Brooke with his body. "You're out of line, Mrs. Goodman. Your daughter is a grown woman. She's a gifted artist, and she's being paid to use that talent for the good of the community. I won't have you bullying her."

"Who the hell are you to talk to me that way?" Margaret shrieked. "I'll have you fired on the spot. Wait until Gus Slade hears about this. You'll never work in this town again."

The whole thing might have been funny if it wasn't so miserably tragic. Brooke's mother was used to getting her way with threats and intimidation. Her face was ugly beneath her makeup.

Austin simply ignored her bluster. "I'd like you to leave now," he said politely. "Brooke and I both have work to do for the club, and you are delaying our progress."

Margaret raised her fist…she actually raised her fist.

Austin stared at her.

To Brooke's amazement, her mother backed down. She dropped her arm, turned on her heel and simply walked away.

"Oh my God, you've done it now." Brooke felt her legs crumpling.

Austin whirled and caught her around the waist, supporting her as she went down. She didn't faint, but she sat down hard on the grass and put her head on her knees. "She's going to make your life a living hell."

"Sounds like you know something about that." He

crouched beside her and stroked her back, his presence a quiet, steady comfort after the ugly scene.

"I appreciate your standing up for me, but you shouldn't have done it. She doesn't make idle threats. She'll try to get you fired."

"I've dealt with bullies before. But I confess that I've never had to deal with it in my own home. I'm sorry, Brooke."

She wiped her eyes and sniffled, too upset to be embarrassed anymore. "I've applied for six different jobs here in Royal since I finished school, and in every instance I got some flimsy excuse about why I wasn't qualified. The first couple of times I wrote it off to the fact that I was straight out of college and grad school and had no experience, but then I got turned down for a waitressing gig at a place where one of my friends worked. I knew she had put in a good word for me." She released a quavering breath. "So I couldn't understand what I had done wrong…how I had interviewed so poorly that they didn't want me."

"Did you ever find out what happened?" he prodded gently.

"Yes. I couldn't let it go, so I screwed up my courage and went back to the restaurant and talked to the manager. He admitted that my mother had called him and threatened him."

"Son of a bitch."

Austin's vehement shock summed up Brooke's reaction in a nutshell. "Yep. Who does that to their own kid?"

"What exactly is it that she wants you to do?"

"Daddy would be happy if I went to law school and joined him in his firm. Mama is Maverick County royalty. Her family owns one of the richest ranches in Texas. I'm supposed to play the part of the wealthy socialite. Wear the right clothes. Hang out with the right people. Marry the right man."

He grimaced. "Sounds wretched."

"You have no idea. And my mother is relentless. I have an inheritance coming to me from my grandmother's estate when I turn thirty. All that's necessary for me to get my money sooner is to be married or to have my parents' permission. But my mother has convinced my father not to let that happen." She lifted her chin. "So I've decided I'll do whatever it takes to get out from under their roof. This job is the first step toward my liberation. Alexis isn't afraid of my mother. This is real employment with a real paycheck."

"But it won't last long, surely."

"No. The garden part will only take a few weeks. After that, Alexis wants me to do the walls in the childcare center. I'm saving every penny so I can rent an apartment."

He put the back of his hand to her cheek and gazed down at her in concern. "You don't look good, honey. Maybe you should go home."

Brooke struggled to her feet. "Absolutely not. I won't let Alexis down."

He sighed. "When do you quit for the day?"

"Around four."

"How about afterward we grab some food and take

a picnic out in the country...find a quiet place where we can talk?"

"What if someone sees us and asks questions?"

His grin was remarkably carefree for a man who had recently tangled with the Goodman matriarch. "Let's live dangerously."

Five

Gus peered through the French doors and frowned when he spotted Brooke Goodman getting chummy with Austin Bradshaw. He'd have to nip that in the bud. Austin was on his radar as the perfect match for Alexis, even if neither of them knew it yet.

Impulsively, he strode out to the parking lot and climbed into his truck. There was one person who shared his goals, one woman who would understand his frustration. He drove out to Rose Clayton's Silver C Ranch feeling more than a little regret for all the years of bitterness and recrimination that lay between him and Rose. She had hurt him badly when he was a young man. Betrayed him. Broken his heart.

Still, five decades was a long time to carry a grudge. The only reason they were speaking now was be-

cause they were both determined to keep their grandchildren from *hooking up*. Wasn't that what the kids
called it these days?

Hell would freeze over before Gus Slade would let
his beloved granddaughter Alexis marry a Clayton.

Rose answered the door almost immediately after
his knock. She had aged well, her frame slim and regal.
Chin-length brown hair showed only a touch of gray
at the temples. Her gaze was wary. "Gus. Won't you
come in?"

He followed her back to the kitchen. "I found a good
prospect for Alexis," he said.

Rose waved him to a chair and poured him a cup of
coffee. "Do tell."

"His name is Austin Bradshaw. Architect. Widower.
Did some work for me a few years back…a handsome
lad."

"And what does Alexis think?"

Rose's knowing smile irritated him. "She doesn't
know my plans for the two of them yet, but she will. I
need some time, that's all. As long as you keep Daniel
occupied, we'll be fine."

"You can rest easy on that score. I'm sure there will
be any number of eligible women bidding on him at the
bachelor auction."

Gus drained his cup and leaned his chair back on two
legs. "Did Daniel actually agree to the auction thing?
It doesn't sound like his cup of tea."

Rose's face fell. "Well, I had to coax him. I did point
out that he and Tessa Noble would make a lovely couple,
if she bids on him."

"I agree. Makes perfect sense."

"Unfortunately, Daniel gets quite frustrated with me when I try to give him advice about his love life. He has come very close to telling me to stay out of his business. Imagine that. His own grandmother."

Gus snorted. "The world would run a lot more smoothly if young people did what their elders told them to."

Rose went white, her expression agitated. "You don't know what you're talking about, old man."

Her demeanor shocked him. "What did I say, Rose?" The change in her was dramatic. He felt guilty and didn't know why.

"I'd like you to leave now. Please."

Her startling about-face stunned him. He thought they had worked through some of their issues. After all, she had wronged *him*, not the other way around. Was she implying somehow that she had been manipulated by her father? Gus had worked for Jedediah Clayton. To a sixteen-year-old kid, the ranch owner had been both vengeful and terrifying. Yet that hadn't stopped Gus from falling in love with the boss's daughter.

Gus had finally made the decision to leave the Clayton ranch. He'd spent four years on the rodeo circuit, saving every dime. Then he'd returned to Royal, bought a small parcel of land and gone back to claim the woman he loved.

His world had come crashing down when he discovered his childhood sweetheart had married another man. Even worse was Rose's crushing rejection of the love they had once shared. The long-ago heartache was still vivid to him.

He had married her best friend.

But now he was confused.

"Go," she cried, tears gleaming in her eyes.

He caught her hands in his and held them tightly, even when she tried to yank away. "Did your father do something to you, Rosie?" His heart sank.

Her lower lip trembled. Suddenly, she looked every one of her sixty-seven years. "None of you cared," she whispered. "I was a prisoner, and you and Sarah never saw through my facade."

"I don't understand." His chest hurt. He couldn't breathe.

"He threatened me. My mother was desperately ill. He was going to let her die if I married you, refuse to pay for her treatments. So I had no choice. I had to pretend. I had to choose my mother's life over my happiness. I had to marry another man."

"My God."

Rose stared at him, her eyes filled with something close to hatred and loathing. Or maybe it was simply grief. "Go, Augustus. We'll continue our plan to keep Daniel and Alexis apart. But please don't come to my house again."

Somehow Brooke managed to work on her mural hour after hour without passing out or giving up, but it wasn't easy. The episode with her mother had upset her deeply. She felt wretched. Even now, her legs trembled and her stomach roiled. Her life was a damned soap opera. Why couldn't her family be normal and boring?

She paused in the middle of the day to eat the peanut butter sandwich she had packed for her lunch. The club had a perfectly wonderful restaurant, but dining there would have meant changing out of her paint-stained clothes, and Brooke simply didn't have it in her today. So she sat on the ground with her back to the wall and ate her sandwich in the shade.

She half hoped Austin would show up to keep her company. But clearly, he was very busy with the new project. She saw him at a distance a time or two. That was all.

On the one hand, it was good that he didn't hover. She would have hated that. She was a grown woman. Still, she'd be lying if she didn't say she was looking forward to their picnic.

By the time she finished a section at three thirty and cleaned her brushes, she was wiped out. Today's temperature had been ten degrees above normal for mid-October. It was no wonder she was dragging. And she had forgotten to wear sunscreen. So she would probably have a pink nose by the end of the day.

She stashed her supplies in her car, changed out of her work clothes into a cute top and jeans, and went in search of Austin. Her palms were damp and her heart beat faster than normal. The last time the two of them had spent any amount of time together, they'd been naked.

Despite that anomaly, they really were little more than strangers. Perhaps if she treated this picnic as a first date, she could pretend that she hadn't propositioned him in a bar and made wild, passionate love to the handsome cowboy.

That was probably impossible, given the fact that she trembled every time he got close to her.

She rounded a corner in the gardens and ran straight into the man who occupied her tumultuous thoughts.

He steadied her with two big hands on her shoulders. "Slow down, honey. I was just coming to find you."

She wiggled free, trying not to let him see how his touch burned right through her. "Here I am. Shall we swing by the corner market and pick up a few supplies for our picnic?"

Austin took her elbow and steered her back inside the club, down the corridor and out the front door. "I've already got it covered," he said. "I called the diner and had them make us a basket of fried chicken and everything to go with it."

Brooke raised an eyebrow. "I'm impressed." The Royal Diner was one of her favorite places for good old-fashioned comfort food. "I hope you asked for some of Amanda Battle's buttermilk pie."

Austin grinned. "I wasn't sure what kind of dessert you preferred, so I had them include four different slices."

"I like a man with a plan."

They were flirting. It was easy and fun. Something inside her relaxed for the first time all day.

Of course, it made sense to take Austin's truck. It was the nicer, bigger, newer vehicle. He stepped into the diner to pick up their order, and then they were on their way. It was a perfect fall afternoon. The sky was the color of a Texas bluebonnet, and the clouds were soft white cotton balls drifting across the sky.

Brooke was content to let Austin choose their route until it occurred to her that he didn't live in Royal. "Do you even know where you're going?" she asked.

"More or less. I did a big job for Gus some years ago. It's been a little while, but this part of the county has stayed the same."

They drove for miles. The radio was on but the volume was turned down, so the music barely intruded. Brooke sighed deeply. She hadn't realized how tightly she was wound.

Austin shot her a sideways glance. "Has your mother always been like that?"

"Oh, yeah."

He reached across the small space separating them and put a hand on her arm. Briefly. Just a touch of warm, masculine fingers. But the simple gesture made her nerves hum with pleasure.

"Tell me why you came to Joplin that night," he asked softly.

"It was a stupid thing to do," she muttered.

"You don't hear me complaining."

The sexy teasing made her cheeks hot. "I was furious at my parents and furious at myself. Some people might have gotten stinking drunk, but that's not my style."

"So you decided to seduce a stranger."

"I didn't seduce you…did I?"

He parked the truck beneath a lone cottonwood tree and put the gear shift in Park. Half turning in his seat, he propped a big, muscular arm on the steering wheel and faced her. He chuckled, scratching his chin and shaking his head. "I don't know what else you would call it. I came in with my sister and left with you."

"Oh." When you put it like that, it made Brooke sound like the kind of woman who could command a man's interest with a crook of her finger. That was certainly never an image she'd had of herself. She kind of liked it. "Well," she said, "the thing is, I was upset and angry, and I let myself get carried away."

"Had something happened at home? Was that it? After what I witnessed today, I can only imagine."

"You're very perceptive. It's a long story. Are you sure you want to hear it?"

He leaned over without warning and kissed her. It was a friendly kiss. Gentle. Casual. Thrilling. His lips were warm and firm. "I've got all night."

She blinked at him. He sat back in his seat as if nothing out of the ordinary had happened. Her toes curled in her shoes. "Well, okay, then." It was difficult to gather her thoughts when what she really wanted to do was unbutton his shirt and see if that broad, strong chest was as wonderfully sculpted and kissable as she remembered.

"Brooke?"

Apparently she had lapsed into a sex-starved, befuddled stupor. "Sorry. I'll start with Grammy, my dad's mother. She died when I was seventeen, but she and I were soul mates. It was Grammy who first introduced me to art. In fact, when I was twelve, she took me with her to Paris, and we toured the Louvre. I remember walking through the galleries in a daze. It was the most extraordinary experience. The light the artists had captured on canvas...and all the colors. The sculptures. Something clicked for me. It was as if—for the first time in my life—I was where I was supposed to be."

"She must have been a very special lady."

"She was. I was crushed when she died, utterly heartbroken. But I made several decisions over the next few years. First, that I wanted to become an artist. And secondly, that I wanted to take part of my inheritance and tour the great art museums of Europe in Grammy's honor."

"And was there more?"

She smiled, for the moment actually believing it might happen. "Yes. Yes, there was...there *is*. I want to open an art studio in Royal that caters to children and youth. Families pay for piano lessons and ballet lessons and soccer and football all the time. Yet there are tons of children like me who need a creative outlet, but their parents don't know what to do for them."

"I think that's a phenomenal idea."

"I did, too. I even went to the bank and filled out the paperwork for a small business loan to get things started. My inheritance would serve as collateral, but I was hoping my parents would see the sense in letting me have part of the money now as an investment in my future."

"I'm guessing they didn't share your vision."

She shook her head and swallowed against the sudden dryness in her throat. "I might have swayed my father...eventually. But my mother was outraged, and he does whatever she tells him to. That ugly scene went down the day I showed up in Joplin."

"Ah. So you were trying to punish them?"

"No. It wasn't that. I was just so very tired of them controlling my life. I'm sure you think I'm exaggerating or overreacting, but I'm not. Did you know that my brother was engaged to be married recently? His poor fiancée, Shelby, ran away from the church, and then my parents tried to blackmail her into coming back by freezing all her assets and hunting her down like an animal."

"Good Lord."

"I know! It's Machiavellian."

"Come on, darlin'," Austin said. "We need to take your mind off your troubles. Let's get some fresh air."

Brooke climbed out of the truck and stretched. Actually, she had to jump down. Being vertically challenged meant that half of the vehicles in Royal were too big for her to get in and out of comfortably.

The thing about an impromptu picnic was that a person couldn't be too picky. Instead of an antique quilt smelling of laundry detergent and sunshine, Austin grabbed a faded horse blanket from the back.

"I think this is fairly clean," he said.

They spread the wool blanket beneath the tree and anchored one corner with the wicker basket. The diner had recently begun offering these romantic carryout meals for a small deposit.

Austin handed her one container at a time. "Here you go. See what we've got." Brooke's stomach rumbled as the wonderful smells wafted up from the basket.

The meal was perfect, but no more so than the late-afternoon sunshine and the ruggedly handsome man at her side. She fantasized about what it would be like to kiss him again. Really kiss him.

Austin ate in silence. His profile was unequivocally masculine. Lounging on one elbow, he personified the Texas cowboy, right down to the Stetson.

"Will you tell me about your wife?" Brooke asked.

Austin winced inwardly. He'd been expecting this question. Under the circumstances, it was a reasonable request, and nothing about Brooke's tentative query reflected anything but concern.

The diner was famous for its fresh-squeezed lemonade. It was served in retro-looking thermoses that kept the liquid ice-cold. Austin drained the last of his and set it aside. Wiping his hands on his jeans, he sat up and rested his forearms on his knees. "Jenny was the best. You would have liked her. She had a big heart, but she had a temper to match. When we were younger, we fought like cats and dogs." He laughed softly, staring into the past. "But the making up was always fun."

"Where did you meet?"

"College. Pretty ordinary love story. I always knew I was going to be an architect. Jenny was in education. She taught high school Spanish until she got sick."

"When was that?"

"We'd been married almost five years and were living in Dallas. She had a cold one winter that never seemed to go away. We didn't think anything about it. But it got worse, and by the time I made her go to the doctor, the news was bad. Stage-four lung cancer. She'd never smoked a day in her life. None of her family had. It was a rare cancer. Just one of those things."

"I'm so sorry, Austin."

He shook his head, even now feeling the tentacles of dread and fear left over from that time. "We went through two years of hell. The only saving grace was that we hadn't started a family. Jenny was so glad about that. She didn't want to leave a child behind without a mother."

"But what about you?" Brooke said, her gray eyes filled with an ache that was all for him. "Wouldn't a baby have been a comfort to you?"

He stared at her. No one had ever asked him that. Not Jenny. Not Audra. No one. Sometimes—way back then—the thought had crossed his mind. The idea of holding a baby girl who looked like Jenny—teaching her to fish when she was a little kid—had rooted deep inside him, but then the chemo started and fertility was a moot point.

"It wouldn't have worked out," he said gruffly. "What did I know about babies?"

"I suppose…"

"In the end, Jenny was ready to go, and I was ready to let her go. There are some things no one should have to endure. She fought until there was no reason to fight anymore." He swallowed convulsively. "When it was over, I didn't feel much of anything for a few days. Nothing seemed real. Not the funeral. Nothing. I didn't even have our house to go back to."

"What happened to your home?" she asked quietly.

"When Jenny's disease had progressed to the point that I couldn't work and care for her, we sold everything and moved to Joplin. Audra and I cobbled together a schedule for looking after Jenny and filled in the gaps with temp nurses and hospice toward the end."

"You and your sister are close."

"She saved my life," he said simply. "I don't know what I would have done without her. I had no rudder, no reason to get out of bed in the mornings. Audra forced me into the world even when I didn't want to go. Eventually, I started picking up work here and there. I didn't mind traveling."

"But what about your career in Dallas?"

"It had been too long. I didn't want to go back there. But Joplin was where Jenny died, so I didn't want to live there, either."

"Then you've bounced around?"

He nodded slowly. "For six years. Pathetic, isn't it?"

Brooke scooted closer and laid her head on his shoulder. "No. I can't imagine loving someone that much and losing them."

He wrapped an arm around her waist and inhaled the scent of her hair. Today it smelled like strawberries. Arousal curled in his gut, but it simmered on low, overlaid with a feeling of peace. It had taken him a long time, but he had survived the depths of despair. He would never allow himself to be that vulnerable again.

"Brooke?" he said quietly.

"Yes?"

"I know you're feeling sorry for me right now, and I don't want to take advantage of your good nature."

She pulled back and looked up at him. Her hair tumbled around her shoulders, pale gold and soft as silk. A wary gray gaze searched his face. "I don't understand."

"I want you." He laid it out bluntly. There didn't need to be any misunderstandings between them. If she was interested in a sexual liaison with him, he was definitely on board, but he wouldn't be accused of wrapping things up in romantic words that might be misconstrued.

Brooke frowned. "I heard you say very clearly that you weren't interested in a relationship."

He rubbed his thumb across her lower lip, tugging on it ever so slightly. "Men and women have sex all the time without relationships. I like you. We have chemistry in bed. If you're interested, I'm available."

Six

Brooke stepped outside her body for a moment. At least that's how it seemed in that split second. The scene was worthy of the finest cinema. A remote setting. Romantic accoutrements. Handsome cowboy. Erotic proposition.

This was the part where the heroine was supposed to melt into the hero's arms, and if it were a family-friendly film, the screen would fade to black. The trouble with that scenario was that Brooke didn't see herself as heroine material in this picture.

You had the leading man who was most likely still in love with his dead wife. A second woman who was far too young for him—case in point, she was having trouble extracting herself from under her parents' oppressive influence. And a red-hot, clandestine one-night stand that had catapulted an unlikely couple way too far in one direction and not nearly far enough in another.

Brooke knew the size and shape of the mole on Austin's right butt cheek, but she had no idea if he put mayo on his roast beef sandwiches.

That was a problem.

She tasted his thumb with the tip of her tongue, her heart racing. How bad could it be if she had naughty daytime sex with this man? He needed her, and that was a powerful aphrodisiac.

Putting a hand on his denim-clad thigh, she leaned in and kissed him. "I could get on board with that idea."

A shudder ripped its way through Austin's body. She felt it. And she heard his ragged breathing. "Are you sure? What changed your mind?"

She reached up and knocked his Stetson off his head. "I'm sure. I can't resist you, Cowboy. I don't even want to try."

They were parked beside a wet weather stream. The land was flat for miles in either direction. No one was going to sneak up on them.

Austin eased her onto her back. "I need to tell you something."

Alarm skittered through her veins. "What is it?

He leaned over her, his big frame blocking out the sun. "I haven't slept with any other women since you. I was serious when I said I'm not looking for a relationship. But I didn't want you to think you were one in a long line."

"Thank you for telling me that."

She couldn't decide if his little speech made her feel

better or worse, but soon, she forgot to worry about it. Austin dispatched her clothes with impressive speed and prowess. The air was cool on her belly and thighs. When she complained, he only laughed.

He sheathed himself, came down between her legs and thrust slowly. Oh, man. She was in deep trouble.

Austin Bradshaw was the real deal. He kissed her and stroked her and moved inside her as if she were his last chance at happiness and maybe the world was even coming to an end. That was heady stuff for a woman whose only real boyfriend had lasted barely six months…during senior year in college.

She wrapped her legs around his back. Her fingers flexed on his warm shoulders. He had shed his shirt and his pants, but he was still wearing socks. For some odd reason, that struck her as wildly sexy.

Sex had never seemed all that special to her. Oh, sure, she thought about it sometimes. When she was lonely or bored or reading a hot book. But her life was full and busy, and the only experience she'd had up until two months ago had convinced her that the movie version of sex was not realistic.

As it turned out, that was true.

Sex with Austin Bradshaw was way *better* than the movies.

He nibbled the side of her neck right below her ear. "Am I squashing you, honey? This isn't exactly a soft mattress at the Ritz."

She tried to catch her breath, but the words still came out on a moan. "No. I'm good. I think there may be a small rock under my right hip bone, but my leg went numb a few minutes ago, so no worries."

"You should have said something." He rolled to his back, taking Brooke with him.

"Oh, gosh." Now she was on top. Exposed. Bare-assed naked. In the daytime. Well, the sun was *trying* to go down, but there was still plenty of light if anyone was looking.

This was far different from dimly lit motel sex in the middle of the night. Austin noticed, too. He suckled each of her breasts in turn, murmuring his pleasure and sending liquid heat from there to every other bit of her. "I love your body, Brooke. Do you know how beautiful you are?"

How was a woman supposed to answer that? Brooke wasn't a slug. She worked out and she was healthy. But beautiful? She had always wanted to be taller and more confident and to have a less pointy chin. "I'm glad you think so," she said diplomatically.

He bit a sensitive nipple, making her yelp. "If we're going to have sex with each other on a regular basis, you have to promise me you'll love your body." He ran his hands over her bottom, pulling her a little closer against him, filling her incrementally more.

"Yes, sir," she said, kissing his nose and his eyebrows and his beautiful, gold-tipped eyelashes.

He thrust upward. "We'll be exclusive," he groaned. "No one else while we're together. Understood?"

Was he insane? What woman was going to fool around when she had Austin Bradshaw in her bed? Nevertheless, Brooke nodded. A plan began forming in her head, but it was hard to focus on anything sensible when her body was like hot wax.

He gripped her hips tightly and moved her against him. Need flared, hot and urgent and breathless. She was burning up from the inside out, even though parts of her were definitely cold.

It was dusk now. The stars were coming out one by one. Or maybe she was the starry-eyed dreamer. How had she gotten so lucky? Like a rare comet, men of Austin's caliber came around once in a long time. She wouldn't be greedy. She wouldn't ask for more than he had to give.

He kissed her roughly, his lips warm, his breath feathering the hair at her temple where it fell across his face. "I don't want to send you home tonight, Brooke. But I'm staying in one of Gus's bunkhouses. We're gonna have to figure something out."

She nodded again, the speech centers in her brain misfiring. "Working on it," she stuttered. His fingers slid deep into her hair, tipping her head so he could nip her earlobe. He sucked on the tiny gold stud. "You make me want things, honey."

"Like what?" She was breathless, yearning.

"If I tell you, you might run away."

"I won't, I swear."

She ran her hands over his arms. Despite the plummeting temperatures, his skin was hot. His muscles were impressive for a man who called himself an architect. Clearly he did more than wield a pencil all day.

He was barely moving now, his body rigid. His chest heaved. "Damn it."

"What's wrong?" She probably should be alarmed, but she was concentrating too hard on the finish line to care.

"I only have one condom," he growled.

The pique in his voice struck her as funny. "We'll improvise later," she said, laughing softly. "Make me come, Cowboy. Send me over the edge."

Austin Bradshaw was clearly a man who liked a challenge. With a groan, he rolled her beneath him again and pistoned his hips, driving into her over and over until they both went up in a flare of heat. Brooke unraveled first, clutching Austin because he was the only steady point in a spiraling universe.

She was barely aware of his muffled shout and the way he shuddered against her as he came.

It took a long time for reality to intrude. Gradually, her breathing settled into something approaching normal. Her heartbeat dropped below a hundred.

Austin grunted and shifted to one side, dragging her against him. "Damn, girl, you're freezing."

"I don't care," she mumbled, burrowing into his rib cage. The man smelled amazing.

He yawned and lifted his arm to stare at his watch. "It's late."

"Yeah." Apparently, neither of them cared, because they didn't move for the longest time.

Eons later, he stirred. "Is there any food left?"

The man must be starving after burning all those calories. "Probably." Her heart began to race. She had reached a pivotal moment in her life, and she didn't want to screw it up. "Austin?"

"Hmm?"

"I want to ask you a question, but you have to promise me you'll think about it, and you won't freak out."

He chuckled. "I'm feeling pretty mellow at the moment. Ask me anything, honey."

"Will you marry me?"

Austin rolled to his feet and reached for his clothes, panic slugging in his chest. "We need to get in the truck. I think you have hypothermia."

"I'm serious," Brooke said, her voice steady and determined.

"Get dressed before you freeze to death." That was the thing about October. It could be really warm on a nice afternoon, but when the sun went down and the skies were clear, it got cold fast.

They found all their clothing. Between them, they repacked the picnic basket. "We can snack in the truck," Brooke said.

He folded up the blanket and tossed it in the back. They climbed into the cab. The picnic hamper was between them. Austin found a lone chicken leg and munched on it. He wasn't about to say a word at the moment. Not after that bomb she had just tossed at him.

Brooke finished off a bag of potato chips and stared out through the windshield into the inky darkness. "I was serious," she said at last.

"Why?" He could barely force the word from his throat. He'd done the marriage thing, and it had nearly destroyed him.

She reached up and turned on the small reading light

that cast a dim glow over the intimate space. With the doors closed and the body heat from two adults, they were plenty warm now.

Brooke looked tired. She had smudges of exhaustion beneath her eyes and her cheekbones were hollow, as if she had lost some weight. "I'm not in love with you, Austin, and I don't plan to be. You can rest easy on that score. But I could use your help. You told me yourself that you've been bouncing from town to town since your wife died. Royal is as good a place as any to put down temporary roots."

"And why would I do that?"

"To help me get my inheritance. You met my mother today. You saw what she's like. You actually made her back down, Austin. You were the alpha dog, and she respected that. Marry me. Not for long. Six months. Maybe twelve. By then I'll have my inheritance and I can have my art studio up and running."

"What's in it for me?" It was a rude, terrible question, but he was trying to shock her into seeing how outrageous her plan was.

She smiled at him, a surprisingly sweet, guileless smile given the topic of conversation. "Regular sex. Home-cooked meals. Companionship if you want it. But most of all, the knowledge that you're doing the right thing. You're making a difference in my life."

Well, hell. When she put it like that… He cleared his throat, alarmed by how appealing it was to contemplate having Brooke Goodman in his bed every night. "Your parents will go ballistic," he pointed out. "I'm nobody on their radar. To be honest, I'll be seen as a fortune hunter by the whole town. That's not a role I'm keen to play."

She nodded slowly. "I understand that. But my parents have no say in the matter when it comes to marriage. I'm well past the age of consent, and my grandmother's will is very clear. The money is mine if I'm married. As for the other…if it would make you feel better, we could sign a prenup, and I could spread the word that you insisted on having one because you're such a Boy Scout."

"You seem to have thought of everything."

"Not really. The idea only began percolating this morning when I saw how you handled my mother."

"I can't *make* her hand over your inheritance."

"Exactly. That's why I began thinking about a temporary marriage." She reached out and stroked his arm. "You're a good man, Austin Bradshaw. Life has knocked you down once. I won't give you any grief, I swear. We'll make our agreement, and when the time is up, you'll walk away free and clear, no regrets. You have my word."

He looked down at her slender fingers pressed against the fabric of his shirt. Her touch burned, as if it were on his bare skin. Already, he could see the flaw in this plan. Brooke Goodman tempted him more than any woman had since Jenny died. He didn't want to *need* anybody else. He didn't want to crave that human connection. Being alone had been comfortable and safe.

"I'll think about it," he said gruffly. "But don't get your hopes up."

Seven

Austin avoided Brooke for an entire week. He was ashamed to admit it, even to himself, but it was true.

He saw her, of course. Across the courtyard garden. They were both working at the same outdoor location. But he kept his distance. Because he didn't know how the hell he was going to respond to her proposal.

With each hour and day that passed, he wanted more and more to say yes to her wild and crazy idea. That was insane enough to stop him in his tracks.

Fortunately, Gus's job kept Austin legitimately busy. Getting the stage ready in time for the upcoming auction required long hours and plenty of focus. Thanks to having an inside track, the plans were approved by the zoning board immediately. Austin had ordered the materials on the spot, and they had already begun arriving pallet by pallet. Soon, the first saws would start humming.

Gus had hired a foreman, but Austin was the boss. He liked the hands-on aspect of the project, and he was a bit of a control freak. It was his design, his baby. In the end, any problems would fall to him. He intended to make sure everything was perfect.

It amused him to realize that a number of the club members had taken to dropping by during the week to gauge the progress on the new stage addition. At first he thought it was to check up on him. Later, he realized that most of them, the men in particular, were simply interested.

One of the younger guys, Ryan Bateman, turned out to be very friendly. He even wrangled Austin into joining a pickup basketball game one evening. After that, when Austin was still avoiding Brooke later in the week, Ryan issued a lunch invitation.

"Let's eat in the club dining room," the other man said. "My treat. I think I know someone who could throw some work your way. You'll like him a lot."

"I don't know that I'm planning on staying in Royal," Austin said, wondering if Brooke had put Ryan up to this. Ryan was a club member, of course. Austin was not.

"At least come for the free food," Ryan chuckled. "What could it hurt?"

Austin glanced down ruefully at his dusty work clothes. "I'm not exactly dressed for the club dining room."

Ryan shook his head. "No worries. The old-school

days with the rigid dress code are long gone—well, at least during lunchtime."

The other man looked pretty scruffy as well, to be honest. He had a day's growth of beard, and his green eyes twinkled beneath shaggy brown hair. His broad shoulders stretched the seams of a plain navy Henley shirt.

"A decent meal sounds good," Austin said, giving in gracefully. "Let me wash up, and I'll meet you inside."

At the end of the building where he was working, there was an outdoor faucet. He shoved his shirtsleeves to his elbows and threw water on his face and arms. Using a spare T-shirt to dry off, he tucked his white button-up shirt into his ancient khakis and scraped his hands through his hair. Rich people didn't spook him. They had their problems, same as anybody else.

Up until now, he'd been swinging by the convenience mart at the end of town each morning and picking up a prepackaged sandwich for his lunch so he didn't waste time on a midday meal. But he had to admit, he was looking forward to something more substantial.

Ryan was leaning against a wall in the hallway waiting on him. The two men made their way into the dining room where a uniformed maître d' seated them at a table overlooking the gardens. Except for a variety of chrysanthemums and a few evergreens, the area was dull and brown. Presumably the landscapers would bring in some temporary plants and foliage for the auction, ones that could be whisked away for the winter.

Just as they got settled, another club member joined them. If Ryan and Austin were on the scruffy side, this guy was a young George Clooney who had just stepped off his yacht. He was easily six foot three. Black hair. Blue eyes. A ripple of feminine interest circled the dining room.

Ryan grinned broadly. "Austin, meet Matt Galloway. Matt, Austin Bradshaw. Austin is new in town. He's the architect Gus hired to do the stage addition out in the gardens."

Matt shook Austin's hand. "It's a pleasure. I like what you've done so far out there."

"Thank you," Austin said. "Are you a cattle rancher like Ryan here?"

Ryan snorted. "Not hardly. Galloway is an oil tycoon. And did I mention that he's newly engaged?"

Despite his sophisticated appearance, Matt's sheepish smile reflected genuine happiness. "I am, indeed."

Austin smiled. "Congratulations."

Ryan summoned the waiter. "A bottle of champagne, please. We need to toast the groom-to-be."

While they placed their lunch orders and waited for the drinks to be poured, Ryan pushed his agenda. "Austin, Matt's going to be needing a house. Tell him, Matt."

Matt nodded. "My fiancée and I do want to build. We have ideas, but neither of us has the skill set to get our vision on paper, so to speak. I was hoping you might be the person to help us."

Austin frowned slightly. "The stage addition is hardly a true showcase of my work. You do realize that, right?"

"Of course." Matt grinned. "But Ryan here is a pretty damn good judge of character, and if he likes you, that's good enough for me. Rachel and I want someone we feel comfortable with, someone who can guide us without taking over."

"I don't even know if I'm planning on sticking around," Austin admitted, feeling the sand eroding beneath his feet.

Ryan jumped in. "Where's home?"

"Dallas originally. And I've spent time in Joplin."

Matt paused as the waiter delivered their appetizers. "Are you footloose and fancy-free like Bateman here?"

Austin hesitated. He never knew quite how to answer this question. "I was married," he said simply. "But my wife died some years back. Cancer. I've moved around since then."

Ryan sobered. "Sorry, man. I didn't know."

Matt stared at him. "I'm sorry, too. But I have to tell you, Royal is a great place to live. Maybe it's time to put down a few roots."

"It's possible." Austin flashed back suddenly to a vision of Brooke's naked body and her unexpected proposal.

"Take your time," Matt said. "I'm not in a huge rush. When the auction is done, maybe you could have dinner with Rachel and me and we could kick around a few ideas. No pressure."

Austin nodded slowly. "That's doable. Thank you for the offer, and I'll be in touch."

The conversation moved away from personal topics after that. Austin realized that he had missed the camaraderie with other guys since he had given up his formal career. He had bounced from job to job, keeping to himself and walling off his emotions. Perhaps it was time to let the past go…

Still, it was a hell of a jump from moving on to being stupid enough to put his heart on the line again. Losing Jenny had ripped him in two and nearly made him give up on life. For several years, he had done little more than go through the motions.

He was not the same man he had been before Jenny died.

With an effort, he dragged his attention back to the present. Ryan and Matt seemed to enjoy poking at each other. While they dived into a heated argument about the upcoming World Series, Austin gazed through the large plate-glass window nearby, looking for Brooke. She had finished one entire section of her mural this week. Unicorns and fairies danced with odd little creatures that must be trolls or something like that.

He loved seeing Brooke's art. It gave him an insight into her fascinating brain. Suddenly, there was movement at the far end of the wall on the other side of the garden.

There she was. Her small aluminum stepladder caught the sun for a moment and cast a blinding reflection. He squinted. What the hell? She was working all the way up under the eaves. Surely the club had an extension ladder. Brooke wasn't tall enough to reach that section…was she?

He couldn't really tell from the angle where he was sitting. Austin stood up abruptly, an odd premonition of danger making him jumpy. All three men had finished their meals. Ryan had already signed his name and put the lunches on his account. "I should get back out there," he said. "Thanks for lunch, guys. I'm sure I'll see you around." He shot out of the dining room so fast he was probably being rude, but he couldn't get over the sight of Brooke stretching up on her tiptoes six feet off the ground.

He strode down the hall and through the terrace doors. At first he didn't see her at all. But then he spotted her. After doing his damnedest to ignore her for an entire week, suddenly he felt compelled to hunt her down.

"What do you think you're doing?" he called out, irritation in every syllable.

She looked over her shoulder at him, one eyebrow raised. "Painting a mural." With one dismissive wrinkle of her cute little nose, she returned to her task.

"Don't you think you need a taller ladder?"

"Don't you think you need to mind your own business?"

He counted to ten. "I'm looking out for your well-being."

"That's odd. I could have sworn you've been avoiding me. Why the sudden change?"

The tops of his ears got hot. "I've been busy."

"Uh-huh."

Pale denim overalls cupped her ass in an extremely distracting fashion. Her silky, straight blond hair was caught up in its usual ponytail, but today a streak of blue paint decorated the tips, as if she had brushed up against something.

"I like what you've done so far."

"Super."

"Are you mad at me?"

"I'm not *happy*."

He grinned, feeling better than he had all week. "I've missed you," he said softly.

Brooke turned around on the ladder. It wasn't an easy task. She rested her brush on the open container of paint and stared at him. "I thought you were done with me."

Beneath the flat statement lay a world of hurt. His heart turned over in his chest. "Don't be ridiculous."

She lifted one shoulder and let it fall. "I let you do wicked things to my naked body. And that's the last I saw or heard from you. How would you read that situation?"

"I was thinking about stuff," he protested.

"You mean the marriage proposal?"

He looked around to see if anyone was listening. "Keep your voice down, for God's sake. Of course that's what I mean. You can't throw something like that at a man and expect an answer right off the bat."

"Ah." She looked at him as if he were a slightly dim student. "It doesn't matter anyway," she said. "I've changed my mind. You're off the hook."

"What the hell." He bristled. "I thought I was your best shot?"

She shrugged. "I read the situation wrong. I'm working on a backup plan."

"I didn't even give you an answer."

"My offer had an expiration date," she said, giving him a sweet smile that was patently false. "No need to worry. Your bachelorhood is safe from me."

"You really are pissed, aren't you?"

"I'm nothing, Mr. Bradshaw. You and I are nothing. Now go away and let me work."

With her on the ladder and him on the ground, the conversation was literally not on equal footing. He ground his teeth in frustration. One quick glance at his watch told him now was not the time to push the confrontation to a satisfactory conclusion. "We're not done with this topic," he said firmly. He had people waiting on him. Otherwise, he would have yanked her off that ladder and indulged in a good old-fashioned shouting match. The woman was driving him crazy.

She turned and looked down her nose at him. "It's *my* topic, Austin. You're merely an incidental."

When Austin strode away, his face like a thundercloud, Brooke tasted shame, but only for a moment. She was not a vindictive person. If anything, she leaned too far in the direction of being a people pleaser. But in this case, self-preservation was paramount.

Already her eyes stung with tears and her stomach felt queasy. She was letting herself get in too deep with Austin Bradshaw. Too intimate. Too fast. Too everything.

It was a good thing he hadn't accepted her stupid, impulsive proposal. His heart was ironclad, safely in the care of his dead wife. But Brooke was vulnerable. She liked Austin. A lot. Given enough time, she might fall in love with him. And therein lay the recipe for disaster.

Suddenly, she needed to put some space between them. Even knowing that he was at the far side of the club grounds wasn't enough. She felt wounded and raw. After capping her paint tin and wiping her brush, she climbed down the ladder and headed inside.

Her next project would be painting murals on the inner and outer walls of the club's day-care center. She kept a notepad and pencil in her back pocket. Maybe now was a good time to take a few measurements and begin sketching out ideas for the traditional nursery rhyme motifs she planned to use.

She had already received permission and a visitor's badge to enter the day care itself. Since two classrooms were outside playing, it turned out to be a perfect time for her to eye the walls and brainstorm a bit.

The creative process calmed her. Gradually, she began to feel better. Everything was fine. It was a good thing that he hadn't accepted her proposal. She wouldn't see Austin socially again. It was better that way.

He was clearly on board with the idea of having recreational sex, but Brooke had never been that kind of woman.

Tons of people were. It wasn't that she was a prude. Despite what she'd agreed to the other day in the heat of the moment, though, she simply didn't have the personality to throw herself into a relationship that was strictly physical. She didn't know how to separate emotional responses from physical ones.

Perhaps she was too needy. A lifetime in a family that thought she wasn't good enough had given her some issues. Maybe instead of having hot, no-strings sex, she should find a good shrink.

Was it so wrong to want to be loved without reservation?

When Austin talked about his late wife, she could hear that deep, abiding love in his voice. Even though the end had been horrible, Austin had experienced the kind of relationship Brooke wanted.

Unfortunately, he wasn't keen to get involved again. Which meant that Brooke would be foolish to let herself fall for him. The best thing for her to do was concentrate on her current job and also to keep the bigger picture in focus. Somehow, some way, she was going to make her dreams come true.

She finished up her notes. Realizing she couldn't put off her outside project any longer, she headed for the door, only to run into James Harris, the current president of the TCC. "Hi, James," she said. The two of them were friends and moved in the same social circles, but she hadn't seen him in some time.

"Hey, Brooke." The tall, African American man gave her a smile that was strained at best. Clinging to his leg was a cute toddler about a year and a half, give or take.

"I was so sorry to hear about your brother and his wife." They had been killed in a terrible car accident and had left James custody of their infant son. "That must have been a dreadful time for you."

James exhaled. Lines of exhaustion marked his handsome face. "You could say that. Little Teddy here is a bit of a terror. And to be honest, I don't think I would have agreed to be president of the club if I had known what was coming. I'm barely keeping my head above water. Nannies are coming and going at the speed of light."

Brooke crouched and smiled at the boy. His golden-brown eyes were solemn. She didn't try to touch him but instead spoke in a soft, steady voice, aiming her remarks toward the child's uncle. "You'd be a terror, too, if your world had been turned upside down…don't you think?"

James nodded slowly. "That's true. I know you're right. The poor kid is stuck with me, though, and I know squat about how to care for him. I don't suppose you'd be interested in a job?"

The hopeful light in his eyes, mixed with desperation, made Brooke grin. She stood and squeezed his arm lightly. "Thanks, but no, thanks. I probably know less than you do about kids. Things will get better. They always do."

"I hope so. At least he likes coming here to the day-care center. I kept him at home this morning so he could have a good nap, but I think getting out of the house is good for him. He's incredibly smart."

"See," Brooke said, grinning. "You're already talking like a proud parent."

"But he *is* smart," James insisted.

"I believe you." She brushed Teddy's soft cheek with a fingertip. "Have fun in there, little one. Maybe you'll see me with my paintbrush soon."

James scooped up his nephew and held him close. "I just want to do right by him. What if I screw this up?"

For a moment, she glimpsed his fear. "You won't," she said firmly. "This isn't what you expected from life, James, but we all make adjustments along the way. Deep down, you know that. I have confidence in you.

So did your brother, or he never would have left Teddy in your keeping."

James nodded tersely, as if embarrassed that he had let down his guard even for a moment. "Thanks, Brooke."

She gave him a quick hug. "I've got to get back to my murals. Don't give up. It's always darkest before the dawn and all that."

His grin flashed. "Maybe I'll get you to paint that on one of my stables."

"Don't laugh," she said. "I might just do it."

Eight

Austin stood in the shadows, unobserved, and watched as Brooke said her goodbyes to the man and the boy and headed back outside. He couldn't quite identify the feelings in his chest. None of them were ones he wanted to claim. Was Brooke seriously already moving on in her quest to find a convenient husband?

The wealthy horse breeder was a far more logical match for Brooke than Austin, even on a temporary basis. Gus had introduced Austin to James several days ago and had filled Austin's ear about the current TCC president. James Harris was charismatic, intelligent and a darling of Royal's social scene. To be honest, the guy needed a woman in his life. He had inherited a kid.

Brooke needed a husband. It all made a dreadful kind of sense.

Watching the two of them as they chatted casually told Austin that Brooke was comfortable with the other man. Was she thinking about proposing to James now that Austin had turned her down?

To be fair, Austin hadn't said no. He hadn't said anything at all. He'd been too damned shocked.

He was torn...completely torn. The smart thing to do would be to stay as far away from Brooke as possible until the job was done and he could hit the road again. He was used to being a wanderer now. It was the man he had become.

Even so, something inside him couldn't let Brooke go. Her innocence drew him like a gentle flame. Innocence was more than virginity. Brooke had an outlook on life that Austin had lost. Despite her parents' inability to see her worth, Brooke had not become bitter.

He went back to work, but his brain was a million miles away. Somehow, he had to mend the rift he had caused. Before he did that, he had to decide how to respond to Brooke's shocking request.

He possessed the power to make her life better. She had told him so. Having met her mother, Austin believed that statement to be true.

The only real question was—could he serve as Brooke's pretend husband and still barricade his heart?

Daniel Clayton pulled up at his grandmother's house and cut the engine, leaning back in his seat with a sigh. He loved Rose Clayton and owed his grandmother everything good in his life, but things were getting way too complicated.

After swallowing a couple of headache tablets with a swig of bottled water, he wiped his mouth and got out. The Silver C Ranch was home…always would be. Still, no one had ever told him how the older generation could muck things up.

Knowing he couldn't ignore the summons any longer, he strode up to the porch and rang the bell.

His grandmother answered immediately, looking as if she had just spent several hours at a spa. "Hello, sweetheart. Come on in. I made a pie, and I have coffee brewing." Though she was sixty-seven, she didn't look her age. Her soft voice did little to disguise her iron will. He had both adored her and feared her since he was a child.

They made their way to the warm, inviting kitchen and sat down. While Rose poured the coffee and served the warm apple pastry, Daniel studied his grandmother, wondering why he couldn't just say no to her and be done with it.

He didn't have long to wait. Rose sat down beside him, pinned him with a pointed stare and ignored her dessert. "You haven't had much to say about the upcoming bachelor auction."

"No, ma'am. To be entirely honest, I was hoping I could convince you to get someone to take my place. I really don't want to do it. At all."

"I've told all of my friends that you've agreed to participate."

She said it slyly, using guilt as a sharp weapon. Daring him to protest.

He set down his fork, no longer hungry. "It's not my

thing, Grandmother. I know I said yes, but I've changed my mind."

"The money will benefit the Pancreatic Cancer Foundation, a very worthy cause."

"Then I'll write a check."

"Our family has to be front and center. The Slades are integral parts of this event, and we will be as well."

"So it's a competition."

"Nonsense. I am a long-standing member of the Texas Cattleman's Club and a well-known citizen of Royal. Of *course* I volunteered my dear bachelor grandson for the auction. It was the least I could do. Surely you want to support me in this. And don't forget, I was hoping sweet Tessa Noble might bid on you. That would be a lovely outcome."

Daniel's headache increased despite the medication. He rubbed the center of his forehead. "Please don't try to play Cupid, Grandmother. That never ends well for anyone. Besides, I'm pretty sure Tessa is interested in her best friend, Ryan."

"Ryan Bateman?" Her eyebrows rose.

"Yes. But don't go spreading that around."

"Of course not." His grandmother seemed disappointed.

"I really don't want to do this bachelor thing," he said, trying desperately for one last chance to escape the inevitable.

Her eyes flashed. "Is it because *you're* interested in someone, Daniel?"

His stomach clenched. No matter how he answered,

he was in trouble. And besides, what did it matter now? His love life was toast.

With a big show of glancing at his watch, he stood up and drained his coffee cup. He had barely touched the dessert. "If I can't change your mind, then yes…of course you can count on me."

His grandmother beamed. "You're a wonderful grandson. This will be fun. You'll see."

Brooke painted one last daisy petal and stood back to examine her work. She was proud of what she had accomplished…very proud. So why did the memory of her mother's harsh criticism still sting?

As she was gathering her things in preparation for heading home, she saw a familiar figure striding toward her across the open space that would soon be planted with lush garden foliage. Her heart beat faster. Austin.

Unfortunately, he didn't look too happy. He stopped six feet away and jammed his hands in his pockets. "We need to talk," he declared.

Her heart plunged to her feet. "No," she said. "We really don't. It's okay, Austin. I shouldn't have asked you. It wasn't fair. I'd like to pretend it never happened."

He gave her a lopsided grin. "All of it?"

Her knees went weak. How could he do that to her so easily? Three sexy words and suddenly she was back in his arms, breathless and dizzy and insane with wanting him.

She swallowed. "Be serious."

He inched closer. "You don't look good, Brooke."

"Gee, thanks."

"I'm serious. You're pale and a little green around the gills. Do you feel okay?"

She definitely did *not* feel okay. She was queasy and light-headed. She had been for several days now. But that was nothing, right? "I'm fine," she insisted.

Now he eliminated the last of the buffer between them and took her in his arms. "I'm sorry, Brooke."

His gentle apology broke down her defenses. Her throat tightened with tears. "Someone might be watching from the windows," she choked out.

"I don't really give a damn. Relax, sweetheart. You're so tense it's giving *me* a headache."

She started to shake. A terrible notion had occurred to her this afternoon—a dreadful prospect she had been refusing to acknowledge for the past two weeks. Though it was the last thing she wanted to do, she made herself pull away from his comforting embrace. "I need to go home now. Goodbye, Austin."

He scowled. "You're in no shape to drive. I'll take you."

Hysteria threatened. She had to get away from him. Her stomach heaved and sweat beaded her forehead. "I'll take it easy…roll the windows down. It's not far." Tiny yellow spots began to dance in front of her eyes. "Excuse me," she said, feeling her knees wobble and her hands turn to ice.

With a moan of mortification and misery, she darted into the narrow space where an air-conditioning unit loomed and proceeded to vomit until there was nothing left but dry heaves.

When her knees buckled, strong arms came around

her from behind and eased her to the ground. "I've got you, Brooke. It's going to be okay."

They sat there on the dead grass for what seemed like an eternity. Only the ugly industrial metal protected them from prying eyes. Brooke leaned against Austin's shoulder and stared at an ant who was oblivious to their presence.

He stroked her hair, for once completely silent.

At last, a huge sigh lifted his chest, and he exhaled. "Brooke?"

"Y-yes?"

"Are you pregnant?"

The shaking got worse. "I don't know. Maybe."

Austin cursed beneath his breath and then felt like scum when Brooke went whiter still. He wanted to scoop her up in his arms and carry her to a safe, comfortable place where they could talk, but they were trapped. The three exits at the rear of the property were delivery bays that would be locked by now. The only way out was to march through the French doors, into the club and out the front entrance.

He stroked Brooke's arms, concerned by how cool her skin felt to the touch. "Do you feel like you're going to be sick again?"

She shook her head. "No. I don't think so."

"Can you walk if I keep my arm around you? I can't have you fainting on me."

"I won't faint."

"All we have to do is make it out to my truck. We can we leave your paints here, can't we?"

"I suppose."

He stood and pulled her with him, waiting to see if she really was steady. Brushing her hair back from her face, he bent to look into her eyes. "One step at a time, honey. Look at me and tell me you're okay."

Brooke sniffed. "I'm swell," she muttered. "But don't be nice to me or I'm going to cry all over your beautiful blue shirt."

"Duly noted."

"Get me out of here. Please." Her skin was translucent. Her bottom lip trembled ever so slightly.

Austin wrapped an arm around her waist and said a quick prayer that no one would stop them. He sensed that Brooke was close to the breaking point.

Fortunately, the clock was on their side. They were too early to run into the dinner crowd, and most of the daytime regulars were gone already. Austin whisked his companion inside, down the hall and into the reception area. Other than a few quick greetings and a wave, no one stopped them.

In moments, they were outside on the street. Austin steered her toward his vehicle. When she didn't balk, his anxiety grew. "I think we need some expert advice, Brooke. Do you have a doctor here in Royal?"

Her eyes rounded. "Are you kidding me? I can't walk into some clinic and tell them I might be pregnant. My parents would know before I got back home."

"You're not a child. And besides, there are privacy laws."

"That's cute. Clearly you don't know my mother."

"Then I have a suggestion to make."

Brooke climbed into the passenger seat and covered her face with her hands. "Oh…" The strangled moan made him wince.

"What if we drive over to Joplin? My sister is a nurse. We can talk this over with her."

Brooke wiped her face with the back of her hand, her big-eyed gaze chagrined. "What's to talk about? Either I am, or I'm not."

He kept his voice gentle. "You can't even say the *P* word out loud. Do you want *me* asking the questions, or would you feel more comfortable with another woman?"

"You think I'm an idiot, don't you?"

"No," he said carefully. "But from what you've told me, you haven't been sexually active recently, and I think this thing took you by surprise. I know the condom broke, but you told me you were on birth control."

Her face turned red. "The morning I left the hotel I was so flustered I forgot to take my pill. I didn't realize it until a few days later when I got to the end of the pack and had one left over."

He frowned. "And your period?"

"It started eventually… Well, there was…" She bowed her head. "This is so embarrassing."

"You're saying you had some bleeding."

She nodded, her expression mortified. "Yes."

He drummed his fingers on the steering wheel. "Stay here for a minute. Try to relax. Let me call my sister. I won't mention your name, but I'll ask a few questions."

Without waiting for Brooke to answer, he hopped out of the truck and dialed Audra's number. The conversation that followed was not one a man liked having with his sister, but it was necessary. The longer Audra talked, the more his stomach sank. At last, he got back in the truck.

Brooke was curled in a ball, her head resting on her knees.

He touched her shoulder. "Look at me, honey."

She sat up, her expression wary, and exhaled. "Well, what did she say?"

He shrugged. "According to Audra, you can get pregnant on any day of the month, even if you only miss one pill. It's far less likely, of course, but it happens."

"And the bleeding?"

"It could be spotting from hormonal fluctuations during implantation and not a real period. The only way to know for sure is to take a test."

A single tear rolled down her cheek.

Austin felt helplessness and anger engulf him in equal measures. *This* was exactly why he didn't let himself get involved with sweet young things who didn't know the score. Brooke was vulnerable. She'd been under her parents' intimidating influence for far too long.

To her credit, she'd been doing everything she could to strike out on her own. But the gap between her and Austin was still too great. He was worlds ahead of her in life experience. He knew what it was like to love and to suffer and to lose everything. He wouldn't allow that to happen to him again. Ever.

No matter how much Brooke tugged at his heartstrings, he had no place for her in his life. In his bed, maybe. But only for a season.

So what now?

"I'm sorry," she said, the words dull. "I take full responsibility. This has nothing to do with you."

"Don't be stupid." His temper flared out of nowhere. "Of course it does. I could have said no at the bar. I should have. But I wanted you." He touched her cheek, stroking it lightly. His heart turned over in his chest when she tilted her head and nuzzled her face in his palm like a kitten seeking warmth. He pulled her across the bench seat and into his arms. "Don't be scared, Brooke. We'll figure this out." He paused, afraid to ask the next question but knowing he wouldn't be able to move forward without the answer. "Did you propose to me because you thought you might be pregnant?"

She stiffened in his embrace and jerked backward. Her indignation was too genuine to be feigned. "Of course not. I need my inheritance. That's all."

"Okay. Don't get your feathers ruffled."

She bit her lip. "Oh, hell, Austin. I don't know. Maybe I did. I've been feeling weird for the past week. But I've ignored all the signs. It seemed too impossible to be true. I didn't want it to be true."

They sat there in silence for what seemed like forever. Outside, the sky turned gold then navy then completely dark. Brooke's stomach rumbled audibly.

"Here's what we're going to do," Austin said, trying to sound more confident than he felt. "There's a truck stop halfway between Royal and Joplin. We can get a meal there. It will be reasonably private, and if we're lucky, the convenience mart will have a pregnancy test. How does that sound?"

"Like a bad after-school movie."

He chuckled. The fact that she could find a snippet of humor in their situation gave him hope. "That's my girl. Where's your purse?"

"In my car. One street over and around the corner."

Once they had retrieved what she needed, they set out. Austin tuned the radio to an easy listening station, pulled onto the highway and drove just over the speed limit. His stomach was jittery with nerves.

Brooke was quiet—too quiet. Guilt swamped him, though he had done nothing wrong, not really. Other than not resisting temptation, perhaps.

The truck stop was hopping on this particular night. That was a good thing. Brooke and Austin were able to blend into the crowd. The hostess seated them at a booth with faux leather seats and handed them plastic-coated menus that were only slightly sticky.

Brooke studied hers dubiously.

He cocked his head. "What's wrong?"

"I'm starving, but I'm afraid to eat."

"Start with a few small bites. We've got all night. Or will your parents be expecting you home?"

"No. I told them I was spending the evening with a friend. They don't really care what I do on a small scale. It's the big picture they want to control."

After the waitress took their order, Austin reached across the table and gripped Brooke's hand. "I won't leave you to face this alone," he said carefully. "I need you to know that."

Her eyes shone with tears again. "Thank you."

"Do you want me to go buy the test now and get it over with, or would you rather wait until after dinner?"

She seemed stricken by his question. "Let's eat first. Then maybe we could book a room? Even if we only use it for a couple of hours?" She winced. "OMG. That sounds sleazy, doesn't it?"

The look on her face made him laugh. "I think it's a fine idea. In the meantime, let's talk about your inheritance and what you hope to do with it. I really want to know."

Brooke sat up straighter, and some of the strain left her face. "Well, I told you about starting the art school."

He nodded. "Yes. Do you have a business plan?"

"Actually, I do," she said proudly. "I even have my eye on a small piece of property near the center of town. It's zoned for commercial and residential both, but the woman who owns the land is partial to small-business owners. She and I have talked in confidence, and she really wants me to have it. The only missing piece is capital."

"Which marrying me will provide."

"Exactly."

"Even without a possible pregnancy, I'm surprised you're not more worried about your parents' reactions to me being your fiancé," he said quietly. "I'm not exactly upper-crust. Audra and I have done well for ourselves, but our mom cleaned houses for a living, and our dad was a plumber."

"They're both gone? But you're so young."

"Mom and Dad were never able to have kids. They adopted Audra and me when they were forty-nine. We lost them both within six months of each other last year. Pneumonia."

"I'm so sorry." Her empathy was almost palpable. "That must have been devastating, especially for you. Did it bring back bad memories of losing your wife?"

Nine

As soon as the words left her mouth, Brooke wanted to snatch them back. The flash of bleak remembrance she saw in Austin's eyes crushed her. It was as if the grief was fresh and new. Did he carry it always like a millstone around his neck, or did it come and go only when insensitive friends, like her, for instance, brought it up out of the blue?

Fortunately, the waitress arrived with their meals, and the moment passed.

Brooke, though she was leery of getting sick again, couldn't resist the sight and smell of the comfort food. She was starving and, thankfully, was able to eat without consequences. Austin cleared his plate as well.

The truck stop was as close to a good ole Texas honky-tonk as a place could get. The atmosphere was rowdy and warm and filled with laughter and the scents of cold beer and warm sweat.

It was not the kind of spot Brooke frequented, but tonight, it was perfect. As long as she didn't move from this booth, she was insulated from the consequences of her actions.

Unfortunately, though, the clock continued to move. The check was paid. The evening waned. Though Austin had said little during the meal, his gaze had stayed on her constantly. In his eyes she saw concern and more. Certainly a flash of sexual awareness. They were both thinking about the escapade that had brought them to this moment.

She bit her lip. "Have you heard of Schrödinger's cat?"

Austin sighed. "Here we go."

"What?" she said, indignant.

"Everyone who's ever watched a certain TV sitcom has heard of Schrödinger's cat. You're saying that as long as we sit in this booth and never leave, you're both pregnant and *not* pregnant. Have I got that?"

"Works for me," she said, stirring the melting ice in her Coke moodily.

"You're not a coward, Brooke Goodman. Knowledge is power. One step at a time. I can quote you clichés till the cows come home. Let's go buy that test and see what we're facing."

"It might be negative," she said, desperately clinging to one last shred of hope.

"It might be..."

His impassive expression told her nothing.

The minimart, unlike the truck stop, was *not* crowded. Brooke, her face hot with embarrassment, snatched two boxes—different brands—off the shelf, plunked down her credit card and hastily signed the receipt. Fortunately for her, the employee manning the counter was more interested in his video game than he was in her purchases.

Soon after, Austin secured two keys to room twenty-four, the last unit on the far right end. They parked in front of their home away from home. He unlocked the door and waited for Brooke to enter.

Could have been better. Could have been worse.

The decor was late '80s, but everything appeared to be clean.

She stood, irresolute, in the middle of the floor.

Austin locked the door, took her in his arms and kissed her forehead. "Get it over with. I'll be right here."

The list of humiliating things she had experienced today was growing. Now she had to add peeing on a stick with a tall, handsome cowboy just on the other side of the door. Fortunately, directions for pregnancy tests were straightforward. She read them, did what had to be done and waited.

After the first result, she ripped open the second box. Pee and repeat.

There was no mistaking the perfect match.

She didn't feel like throwing up. She didn't feel anything at all.

Austin knocked on the door. "You okay in there, honey?"

"Yes," she croaked. "Give me just a minute." She

dried them, hoping to erase the evidence. Still the same. Taking a deep breath, she opened the bathroom door and leaned against the frame, feeling breathless and dizzy and incredulous. "Well," she said, "I'm pregnant."

Austin went white under his tan. Which was really pretty funny, because it wasn't exactly a huge surprise. Apparently, like her, he had been hoping against hope that her barfing had been a fluke.

He swallowed visibly. "I see."

"Say something," she begged. Why couldn't this be like the commercials where the woman showed the man the stick and they both danced around the room?

"What do you want me to say?" His gaze was stoic, his stance guarded.

"I keep feeling the need to apologize," she whispered. The tears started then in earnest. They rolled down her cheeks and onto her shirt. Austin didn't want a wife, not even a temporary one. And he surely didn't want a child. This man had been badly hurt. All he wanted was his freedom.

Though she didn't make a sound, her distress galvanized him. He closed the space between them and scooped her up in his arms, carrying her to the bed. He sat down and held her on his lap. "Things happen, Brooke. This situation isn't your fault. It isn't mine."

Time passed. Maybe five minutes, maybe an entire day. So many thoughts and feelings rushed through her body. Having Austin hold her like this was both comforting and at the same time wildly arousing. Her body tensed in heated reaction. In his arms, she felt as if she could handle any obstacle in her path. But at the same time, he made her want things that were dangerous to her peace of mind.

Beneath her, his sex hardened. The fact that Austin Bradshaw was now unmistakably *excited* made her want to strip him and take him without a single thought for the future.

Instead, she scooted off his lap and stood, scrubbing her face with her hands, trying not to compound her mistakes. One thing she knew for sure. "I know I have...options, but I want this baby. Maybe *want* is the wrong word. I'm responsible for this baby. I'm the one who walked into a bar to do something foolish. Now I'm pregnant. So I'll deal with the consequences."

"A baby will change everything about your life," Austin said. His dark gaze was watchful. "It will be a hell of a long time before you can take that monthslong trip to Europe to visit art galleries and study the grand masters."

The enormity of the truth in his words squeezed her stomach. "Yes. But that was a selfish bucket list item and one that can wait indefinitely."

"I'll provide for the child financially. You don't have to worry about money."

She winced. "I appreciate the sentiment, but with my inheritance, that won't be necessary. I'm assuming this pregnancy will tip the balance in my favor. My parents are not fond of babies. They won't want me in the house, so I think they'll have no choice but to turn over what is legally mine."

"Having met your mother, I think you're being naive. If I had to guess, I'd say they'll use your child as a bargaining chip to control you. Your situation hasn't gotten better, Brooke. It's gotten worse."

She gaped at him, studying the grim certainty on his face and processing the truth of his words. "I hadn't thought of it that way."

He stood as well, jamming his hands in his pockets and pacing. "We'll get through this…"

"We?" she asked faintly, feeling as if she were an actor in a very bad play.

He shot her a hard glance, his face carved in planes and angles that suggested strong emotion tightly under wraps. "*We.*" His forceful tone brooked no argument. "We're a family now, Brooke…whether we want to be or not. Our only choice is how to handle the way forward. You asked me to marry you. Now I'm saying yes."

"This isn't your problem," she insisted. "It's *my* baby."

He stopped in front of her, their breath mingling, he was so close. At last, the rigid posture of his big frame relaxed, and a small smile tilted those masculine lips that knew how to turn a woman inside out. "Sorry, honey. It doesn't work that way. There were two of us in that bed."

"But you don't want to be here," she cried. "You're only planning to stay in Royal for a couple of months at the most."

He slid his hands into her hair and cupped her neck, tilting her head, finding her lips with his. "So I'll change my plans," he said, kissing her lazily. "Some women sail through pregnancy. But a lot of them don't. You need someone to care for you and support you. Right now, that someone is going to be me."

Kissing Austin was never what she expected. He could take her from gentle bliss to shuddering need in a heartbeat. Tonight, he gave her something in between. He held her and made her believe, even if for only a moment, that everything was going to turn out okay.

She rested her cheek against his chest, feeling and hearing the steady *ka-thud* of his heartbeat. "I can't ask you to do that." Even if the prospect of having Austin in her corner made her soul sing.

"You don't really have a choice." When he chuckled, the sound reverberated beneath her ear. He was so big and hard and warm. Nothing in her life had ever felt so good, so perfect.

But the perfection was a mirage. Her heart screamed at her to proceed with caution. Austin was being kind. Honorable. He was the sort of man who did the right thing regardless of the cost.

That didn't mean he wouldn't inadvertently break her heart.

She pulled away, needing physical distance to be strong. "I'll talk to my parents tomorrow. If they agree to give me the inheritance, the baby and I can have a home of our own. You don't even have to be involved."

Austin shook his head, his smile self-mocking. "I'm involved up to my neck, Brooke. And I'm not going anywhere for the moment."

For the moment... Those three words were ominous but truthful. She'd do well to plaster them on her heart, so she didn't get any foolish ideas. Suddenly, her knees felt weak. She staggered two steps toward the bed and sat down hard.

His gaze sharpened. "What's wrong?"

"Nothing. Not really. Just a little light-headed. It will pass."

He crossed his arms over his chest. "Do you want to stay here until morning? I can buy what we need at the convenience mart."

From his expression, she hadn't a clue what *he* wanted to do. Probably run far and fast in the opposite direction.

The prospect of spending the night with Austin, even in this unappealing motel room, was almost impossible to resist. It was easy to imagine making love to him all night long and waking up naked in his arms. Her breath caught.

Austin's gaze narrowed. "Are you sure you're okay? You're all flushed."

"I'm fine."

If she were going to be a mother, she had to start making mature decisions. "We can't stay here," she said slowly. "I need to be at the club tomorrow to work on the murals. And before that, I'll have to face my parents at breakfast and tell them the news."

"Don't you want to give yourself time to get used to the idea first? You've had a shock, Brooke."

"I can't have this hanging over my head. I believe in ripping off the Band-Aid."

"Fair enough." He nodded slowly. "And you won't be alone. I plan on being there beside you when you break the news."

"Oh my gosh, no," she squeaked, already imagining the fireworks. "That's a terrible idea. I'm not going to tell them about you."

"Don't be ridiculous. We've already established that I can handle your mother. Besides, the truth will get out sooner or later. This isn't going to be our guilty secret."

Though she was skeptical, she nodded. "If you insist. But don't say I didn't warn you."

Austin took Brooke home. Dropping her off at her parents' house was more difficult than he had expected. Already he felt possessive. Even if he kept himself emotionally divested, Brooke was the mother of his child. That meant something.

The following morning, he dragged himself out of bed, wondering if she had slept any more than he had. A shower did little to offset the effects of insomnia. He shaved and dressed carefully, not wanting to give the Goodmans any overt opportunity to look down their noses at him. Not for his sake, but for Brooke's.

Austin had already seen firsthand how her mother treated her. It didn't take a genius to deduce that a man like Austin would not be on their list of suitable husbands for their daughter.

Brooke had insisted that she be the one to do all the talking, because she knew how to handle her mother and father. Austin had reluctantly agreed.

When he showed up at the imposing Goodman residence, the house looked even more opulent than it had the night before. As an architect, Austin knew plenty about price points and quality building materials. The

Goodmans had spared no expense in building their Pine Valley mansion. He wondered if Brooke had lived here her entire life.

He rang the bell. A uniformed maid answered the summons and escorted him through the house. A full hot breakfast was in the process of being laid out on a mahogany sideboard. Sunlight flooded the room through French-paned windows. The dining table was set with china, crystal and antique silver that sparkled and gleamed.

Brooke greeted him with a smile, though he could see the strain beneath the surface. The elder Goodmans were cool but polite in their welcomes. Once everyone was seated, the grilling commenced.

Simon Goodman eyed Austin with more than a hint of suspicion. "My wife tells me you're doing a temporary job for Gus Slade."

No mistaking the emphasis on *temporary*.

"Yes, sir. Or for the Cattleman's Club, to be more exact. I'm overseeing the outdoor addition to the facilities."

"And you have the suitable credentials?"

Austin swallowed his ire. "An advanced degree in architecture and a number of years' experience at a firm in Dallas."

"But you're no longer with that firm?"

"Daddy!"

Brooke's indignant interruption had no discernable effect on the interrogation. For some inexplicable reason, Margaret Goodman was oddly silent. Austin sighed inwardly. "When my wife became very ill, I worked until she needed constant care, and then I quit my job. Since she passed away six years ago, I've chosen to be a bit of a nomad."

"I can't believe this." Brooke stood up so abruptly, her chair wobbled. She glared at her father. "You're embarrassing me. And you're being horribly rude. Austin is my friend. He doesn't deserve the Spanish Inquisition."

Brooke's mother waved a hand. "Sit down and eat, Brooke. You aren't fooling anyone. Your father is well within his rights to ask as many questions as he sees fit. That's why you've brought Austin here, isn't it? To convince us that you've fallen madly in love with a handyman? And that we're supposed to throw you a lavish wedding and hand over your inheritance?"

The silence that fell was deafening. Scrambled eggs congealed on four plates. Though every bit of the breakfast was spectacularly prepared and worthy of a five-star restaurant, Austin suspected that most of the food would end up in the trash. *He* had certainly lost his appetite. And poor Brooke looked much as she had yesterday when she had gotten sick behind the club.

Every instinct he possessed told him to take charge of the situation, but he had promised to let Brooke do the talking, so he held his tongue. It wasn't easy.

She sat down slowly. Her face was the color of the skim milk Mrs. Goodman was adding to her coffee from a tiny silver pitcher. Brooke cleared her throat. "I was going to broach the subject more gently than Daddy did, but yes, Austin and I are going to get married. We haven't talked about a ceremony yet. I don't even know if I want a big wedding. I'm telling you because you're my parents, not because I expect you to pay for anything."

Poor Brooke looked frazzled. Austin swallowed a bite of biscuit that threatened to stick in his throat. "I am perfectly capable of paying for our wedding. All Brooke needs from you is your blessing and your support. She loves her family and wants to include you."

Austin infused his words with steel. Though it might have gone over Brooke's head given her current physical discomfort, it was clear from Margaret and Simon's expressions that they heard his ultimatum. They could treat Brooke well, or they could lose her...their choice.

Unfortunately, Brooke's mother refused to go down without a fight. "Please understand, Mr. Bradshaw. It's a parent's obligation to protect his or her child from fortune hunters."

The blatant insult was almost humorous. How could sweet, openhearted Brooke have come from such a dreadful woman?

Fortunately, Austin had always relished a good battle. "In that vein, I'm sure you'll understand it's *my* job to make Brooke happy. And by God, that's what I intend to do."

Simon's face turned an ugly shade of puce. "You don't know who you're dealing with, Bradshaw."

"I know that you've blackballed your daughter. That you've made her a prisoner in her own home. That you've deliberately sabotaged her search for meaningful employment. That you've refused to acknowledge she's an adult and one who deserves respect and autonomy."

Margaret slammed her fist on the table. "Get out," she hissed, her gaze shooting fire at him as if she could incinerate him on the spot.

Austin looked across the table at Brooke. He smiled at her, trying to telegraph his unending support and compassion. "Do you want me to go, honey?"

Brooke stood up, seeming to wobble the tiniest bit. She dabbed her lips with a snowy damask napkin and rounded the table to put a hand on his shoulder. "Yes. But not yet. I'll leave with you in a moment."

He heard her take a quavering breath. Now he knew what was coming. Her tension was palpable. Quickly, he got to his feet and put an arm around her waist. Not speaking, just offering his silent support.

Brooke stared at her mother, then her father. She cleared her throat. Her eyes glistened with tears. Austin wanted to curse. This should be a joyful moment. He hated that it was playing out like a melodrama with Brooke's parents as the wicked villains.

"Here's the thing," she said quietly. "Austin and I are getting married. Very soon. After that, I will petition the court for my inheritance. You know it's mine. For you to interfere would be criminal, mean-spirited and petty."

Her fathered puffed out his chest. He glared. "You'll squander every penny in six months. Don't think you can come crawling back for more."

Austin's arm tightened around Brooke. He could literally *feel* the blow of her father's cruel words. "I won't come back home, Daddy," she said. "At least not to stay. I'm a grown woman."

Margaret shoved back from the table and approached

Brooke, using her physical presence as a threat, just as she had in the club gardens. Her smile was cold and merciless. "You're a child. This man doesn't love you. He's using you. All I've ever wanted is what's best for you, baby. Let's put this awful business behind us. Start over. Turn back the clock."

Brooke's spine straightened a millimeter. She slid her hand into Austin's and gripped it so hard her fingernails dug into his skin. "I can't turn back the clock, Mama. I'm pregnant."

Ten

Margaret's infuriated shriek reverberated in the confines of the room. For one terrible moment, Austin thought she was going to strike her own daughter. He thrust Brooke behind him and confronted her mother. "Tread carefully, Mrs. Goodman. There are some bridges you don't want to burn. I think it's best if we continue this conversation at another time."

Without giving anyone a chance to protest, he grabbed Brooke's hand and hurried her out of the room and away from the house. After he hustled her down the front walk to where his truck was parked, he cursed beneath his breath when she leaned against the hood of the vehicle and covered her face with her hands. A pregnant woman needed sustenance. Between morning sickness and emotional trauma, Brooke had barely swallowed a bite as far as he could tell.

He tucked her into the passenger seat and ran around to the other side. Once the engine started, he sighed. Taking her hand in his once again, he lifted it and kissed her fingers. "I am so very sorry, sweetheart."

Brooke shrugged, her gaze trained somewhere beyond the windshield. "It's nothing new. Not really."

"I have a proposition for you," he said, wanting desperately to erase her sorrow.

"Isn't that what got us into this mess?" she said wryly.

Something inside him eased. If she could joke about it, even now, all was not lost. "You can't stay there anymore, Brooke. It's not healthy for you or the baby. Gus has been hosting me in the bunkhouse out at the ranch, but frankly, that's getting old. I've taken a look at some new rental condos on the east side of town. They're really nice. What if we go right now and sign a twelve-month lease?"

Her eyes rounded. "*Live together?*"

"You already proposed to me. This seems like a logical step."

Her face turned pink. "I'm sorry I've complicated your life."

"Stop it," he said. "And relax. Stress isn't good for a woman who's expecting. If nothing else, my job is to pamper you and make sure you have a healthy pregnancy. We enjoy each other's company. What do you say?"

* * *

Half an hour later, Brooke took slow, shallow breaths and tried to convince herself she wasn't going to barf. After escaping the uncomfortable breakfast with her parents, she and Austin had used the drive-through at a fast food restaurant and picked up sausage biscuits and coffee.

They sat in the parking lot and ate the yummy food, barely speaking. Even so, the silence was comfortable. Austin didn't *crowd* her. Most men in this situation would be demanding an answer.

He finished his meal and crumpled up the paper wrapper. "How's your stomach?"

She held out her hand and dipped it left and right. "So-so."

"I can't read your mind, honey. What are you thinking?"

"Honestly?" She grimaced. "As soon as you and I look at condos together, the gossip will be all over town."

"Doesn't change anything, does it?"

"I can't afford to rent a condo. I don't have any money, Austin," she said bluntly. "And even if we were to get married today, the process to claim my inheritance would take longer than you think to work its way through the court system."

"Forget about that," he said, his voice quiet but firm. "I've lived very frugally for six years. I've got money in the bank. Plenty for you and me and the baby."

She felt her face heat. "I've tried so hard to be independent. This feels like a step backward."

"Not at all. This is *us* making a home for our baby. If you don't leave that house, your parents will only find more ways to make your life miserable and to try and control you."

"I want to be clear about our expectations," Brooke said slowly. "Are you suggesting cohabitation or marriage or both?"

His expression shuttered suddenly, every nuance of his real feelings erased. That sculpted masculine jaw turned to granite. "This would be a practical marriage partnership between two consenting adults. I was considering your proposal even before we found out you were pregnant. Now, it makes sense all the way around. Once the baby comes and you're back on your feet physically, emotionally and financially, we'll reassess the situation."

"You mean divorce."

He winced visibly. "That's what you suggested earlier, yes. But even if we separate, I'll always be part of your life on some level. Because of the child."

So clinical. So sensible. Why did his blunt, rational speech take all the color and sunshine out of the day?

"What will you do when the project at the club is finished?"

"Matt Galloway has talked to me about building a house for him. That would take the better part of a year. After that, I don't know. I suppose I may want to stay in Royal because of the baby. I can't imagine not seeing my son or daughter on a regular basis."

And what about me? She wanted him to tell her how hard it would be to walk away from *her*.

Swallowing all her nausea and her misgivings and the pained understanding that Austin was offering so much less than forever, Brooke summoned a smile. "Okay, Cowboy. Let's go look at these condos. Window-shopping doesn't cost a thing."

An hour later, she ran her hand along the window-sill of a cheery, sun-filled room overlooking a koi pond and a weeping willow. The backyard was small but adequate. And it was fenced in. Perfect for a toddler to stagger across the grass chasing a ball or laughing as soap bubbles popped.

This particular condo, the fourth one they had looked at, had three bedrooms—plenty of space for a loner, a new baby and a woman whose life was in chaos. The complex was brand-new, the paint smell still lingering in the air. The rentals were designed primarily for oil company executives who came to Royal for several months at a time and wanted all the comforts of home.

The agent had stepped outside to give them privacy.

Austin put a hand on her arm. "You like it, don't you? I can see it on your face."

She shot him a wry glance over her shoulder. "What's not to like? But these places have to be far too expensive." The units were over three thousand square feet each. They weren't the type of starter homes young newlyweds sought out. Each condo Brooke and Austin had toured was outfitted with high-end everything, from the luxurious marble bathrooms and the fancy kitchens to the spacious family rooms wired for every possible entertainment convenience.

"I told you. Money is not a problem."

Panic fluttered in her chest. "I'll pay you back. Half of everything. As soon as I have my inheritance."

He frowned. "That's not necessary.

"Those are my terms."

Even to her own ears she sounded petulant and ungrateful. But she was scrambling for steady ground, needing something to hold on to, some way to pretend she was in control.

"So we'll get married?" He stood there staring at her with his hands in his pockets and a cocky attitude that said *take me or leave me.*

"You don't have to do this, Austin."

"You promised me home-cooked meals and hot sex."

He was teasing. She knew that. But suddenly, she couldn't make light of their situation. Tears clogged her throat. Creating a home with a baby on the way should be something a man and a woman did that was almost sacred. Brooke and Austin were making a mockery of marriage and family. "I need to visit the restroom," she muttered. "Will you see how long we can wait to give them an answer?"

She locked herself in the nearest bathroom, sat on the closed commode lid and cried. Not long. Three minutes, max. But it was enough to make her eyes puffy. Afterward, she splashed water on her face and tried to repair the damage with her compact.

In the mirror over the sink, she looked haggard and scared. Poor Austin hadn't signed on for all this drama. She used a tissue to wipe away a smudge of mascara and dried her hands on her pants.

Then—because she quite literally had no other

choice—she unlocked the door and went in search of her cowboy.

Austin and the rental agent, an attractive woman in her early forties, were chatting comfortably when Brooke emerged onto the front porch. The other woman gave her a searching look. "Everything okay? I have bottled water in my car."

Brooke nodded. "I'm fine."

Austin curled an arm around Brooke's waist, drawing her close. She leaned into his warmth and strength unashamedly. He smelled good, though his nearness made her knees wobble. She couldn't seem to stop wanting him despite everything that had happened.

The agent eyed them both with a practiced smile. "I was telling Mr. Bradshaw that there are three other couples on the books to see this unit today, two this afternoon and one tonight. As you probably know, decent rental property is hard to come by in Royal. This new development is very popular, and this particular condo was only finished two days ago. This one is outfitted as a model, though you certainly don't have to take the furniture if it's not your taste. If you're interested, though, I wouldn't wait too long."

Austin tightened his arm around Brooke. "Give us a few minutes, would you?"

The woman walked down the steps and out to her car.

"Well," he said. "What do you think?"

Brooke wriggled free, needing a clear head. She couldn't get *that* standing so close to the man who made her breathe faster. He rattled her. "You know it's perfect.

Of course, it's perfect. But that's not really the point. Aren't we rushing into this?"

He lifted an eyebrow. "You're already pregnant. The clock is ticking. You're the one who asked for marriage. I'm happy for the both of us to move in here either way. I'm already imagining all the ways we can use that big Jacuzzi tub."

So could she. The intensity of her need for him made her shiver.

She licked her lips. "I don't think pregnant women are supposed to use hot tubs."

"Then we'll improvise in the shower."

The heat in his gaze threatened to melt her on the spot.

"How can you be so cavalier about the situation?" she cried. There was absolutely nothing she could do about the panic in her voice. The fact that Austin was cool and unruffled told her his emotional involvement was nil. It was Brooke who was unraveling bit by bit.

Austin shook his head slowly. "Take it easy. I didn't mean to pressure you. But it made me so damn mad to see your parents play the bully. Sit, honey. Breathe."

He summoned the agent with a crook of his finger. Brooke sank onto the porch swing, half numb, half scared.

Austin gave the woman a blinding smile. "I'll take it," he said.

The agent faltered. "You?" She glanced at Brooke. "But I thought…"

"The contract will be in my name only," Austin said cheerfully. "Just mine. I asked Ms. Goodman to come along and give me advice. She likes all those flopping and flipping shows, don't you, sweetheart?"

Brooke nodded. Austin was giving her a way out. Was she being a coward? Maybe so. But his gesture touched her deeply, because it told her he understood her fears.

While Austin wrote a check for first and last month's rent and signed a dozen pages of an official-looking contract, Brooke moved the swing lazily, pushing her foot against the crisply painted boards of the porch. Halloween was only a few days away. This house would need a smiling jack-o'-lantern.

Was she going to live here? For real? Or was this some kind of bizarre fantasy?

She tried to imagine it. Coming home each night to Austin Bradshaw. Sharing his bed.

Every scenario that played in her head was more delicious and tempting than the last. Under this roof, she and Austin would be *alone*. She could indulge her lust for his magnificent body over and over and over again. Intimate candlelit dinners for two. Watching movies on the couch and pausing the action on the screen when they couldn't resist touching each other. Lazy Saturday morning sex when neither of them had responsibilities. It would be one long, sizzling affair.

She blinked and came back to reality with a mental thud.

In one blinding instant, she saw the impossibility of her situation. She *did* need Austin. Marrying him would free up her inheritance and thus finance her dreams of owning an art studio in Royal…of training and inspiring the next generation of artists and dreamers.

Marrying him would make her child legitimate in the eyes of the law, an outdated concept no doubt, but one that was nevertheless appealing. Marrying Austin would give her the freedom to finally be her own person.

But at what cost? Living with him would end up breaking her heart.

She watched him as he talked and laughed with the rental agent. He was making a concerted effort to charm the woman, to keep her from spending too much time wondering why Brooke was not signing on the dotted line, as well. Hoping, perhaps, to deflect the inevitable gossip.

Everything about this man was dangerous. From the very first moment Brooke saw him in that crowded bar in Joplin, something about him had spoken to her deepest needs. She was already half in love with him. The only remedy was to stay far, far away.

Instead, she was about to do the exact opposite.

With a sigh, she pulled out her phone and tried to distract herself with emails while she waited for Austin to finish up. At last, the formalities were done. The agent locked up the property and drove away.

Austin sat down beside Brooke and stretched his long arms along the back of the swing. Yawning hugely, he dropped his head back and sighed. "She's going to meet me here at 8:00 a.m. on Monday to pick up the keys. I'll pack my stuff at Gus's this weekend, so I can move in after work that afternoon."

"And me?"

He curled one hand around her shoulder and caressed her bare arm below the sleeve of her top. His fingers were warm against her chilled skin, eliciting delicious shivers. She'd left her jacket in the car, so she snuggled closer, welcoming his body heat.

"Well," he said slowly. "I suppose that's up to you. I hate the thought of you going back to that house."

"It's my home, Austin. They're not going to poison my soup or lock me in my room."

"Don't be too sure. I wouldn't put anything past your mother." He shuddered theatrically. "She scares me."

His nonsense lightened the mood. "Do you really think we can make this work?"

"I do. We're reasonable adults with busy schedules, so we won't be together 24/7. We both have plenty of work ahead of us at the club, not to mention the fact that we have to get ready for a baby. And when it comes to that, by the way, I can be involved as much or as little as you want me to…"

"Okay." She was feeling weepy again. Lost and unsure of herself. Not an auspicious start to a *convenient* relationship. She swallowed. "Are you still willing to marry me?"

His gaze remained fixed out on the street where two delivery trucks were wrangling about parking privileges. "Yes." The word was low but firm.

"Not a church wedding," she said. "Something small. And very simple."

"The courthouse?"

"Yes." Sadness curled in her stomach. If she were

marrying the love of her life, even a courthouse wedding would be romantic. However, under these circumstances, it seemed sad and a bit tawdry.

"I have one requirement."

She stiffened. "Oh?"

He shifted finally, half turning so he could see her face. "I want you to buy a special dress. It's doesn't have to be a traditional gown. But something to mark the day as an occasion. Will you do that for me?"

He leaned forward and brushed her cheek with his thumb. Suddenly, her heart thudded so loudly in her chest she was sure he could hear the ragged thumps. "Yes," she croaked. "I'll go tomorrow."

"Brooke?" He leaned in as he said her name, his lips brushing hers once...twice. "I care about you. I'll never do anything to hurt you, I swear. And I will protect you and this baby with my life."

It was as solemn and sacred a vow as any she had ever heard. Even without the word *love*, it would have to be enough. Austin had already made that other vow on another day with another woman. Brooke would have to be satisfied with these very special promises he had given to her as the father of her baby.

She kissed him softly. "Yes," she said. "I will marry you, and I will live with you. For this one year. And I will do everything in my power to make sure that you don't regret your decision. Thank you, Austin." Curling her arms around his neck, she let herself go, gave herself permission to lower her defenses and simply enjoy the moment.

He wrapped her in his arms tenderly, as if she were

breakable…as if all the passion between them had to be kept in check, muted, held at bay to keep from crushing her. Paradoxically, his gentleness made the moment all the more arousing. Their heartbeats, their longing clashed, and like an almost palpable force, the wanting grew and multiplied.

Emboldened, she slid a hand beneath his shirt and caressed the hard, warm planes of his back.

They were outside. In public. Only the confines of the porch gave them any privacy at all.

Austin groaned.

"What?" she whispered, pressing into him, needing him so badly she shook with it.

"I should have written her a check for three more days and taken the keys right now."

Brooke pulled back and stared at him. "That was an *option*?"

His sheepish smile softened the moment, though not the intensity of her desire for him. On the other side of the door lay at least two brand-new, fully serviceable beds. "I wasn't thinking too clearly. It's not every day a man buys a house for his wife and child."

"Rents," she corrected, reminding herself of the tenuous nature of their agreement.

"Whatever." He glanced at his watch and muttered a curse. His disgruntled expression was almost amusing.

"I take it we're through here?"

He stood and stretched. "I have to meet someone at the club. It's important. Or I wouldn't leave you."

The odd choice of words gave her pause. "I have to go, too. I want to finish up the last outdoor mural so I can start on the daycare walls next week. The weather is supposed to turn dreary."

Austin tugged her to her feet. He rested his forehead on hers. "Will you be here with me Monday night?"

Her heart beat faster. Moving out of her parents' house would be no picnic. "Yes," she said clearly. "You can count on it."

Eleven

They wasted no time in heading for the Texas Cattleman's Club. Austin found a prime parking spot, gave Brooke a quick kiss and ran off for his appointment. She stopped by her own car—still parked where it had been overnight—grabbed a couple of items she needed out of the trunk and went inside to change into her work clothes, engulfed in a haze of giddy anticipation and cautious optimism.

The sun was shining, and the temps were balmy. It was a perfect day to paint, though she missed Austin already. In the distance, she could see the stage addition taking shape. It was going to be a push, but Austin swore he would have everything ready in time for the auction. Already, the landscapers were putting down sod and laying out string and markers for the plants, both temporary and permanent, that would turn the gardens into a fall foliage paradise.

The whole thing was exciting. Not that Brooke would attend the auction itself. At least she didn't think so. She certainly wasn't going to bid on a bachelor. She would, however, make an extremely modest donation to the charity, despite her financial woes. This event was important to Alexis, and Brooke wanted to support her friend in every way she could.

Because she was so close to finishing the entire outdoor project, she opted for peanut butter crackers at lunch. To appease her conscience, she resolved to have a healthy dinner when she got home.

The day flew by. She was in the zone. Anytime her heart was in the midst of a painting, it was as if the brush moved on its own. At four o'clock, she was limp with exhaustion but filled with elation. Two huge outdoor walls now burst with life and color.

As she cleaned up her supplies and packed everything away, she kept an eye out for Austin, but he was nowhere to be found. She told herself not to be silly. Going home to face her parents was something she could do on her own. She didn't need a man to help with that.

In the end, the expected confrontation never materialized. She had completely forgotten that her mother had a huge real estate conference in Las Vegas. Her father had gone along to play golf. Brooke glanced at the calendar in the pantry. They had flown out at 3:00 p.m. Wouldn't be back until Monday night.

She stood in the empty kitchen with an odd feeling

in the pit of her stomach. Instead of facing an unpleasant weekend of arguments and emotional upheaval, all she had to do was pack her things and say goodbye to her childhood home. This time when she walked out, it would be for good.

There were sweet memories in the huge house. Not everything had been a struggle. But unfortunately, the lovelier moments of her childhood had been somewhat obliterated by events in recent years.

The cook had left two different casseroles in the fridge. Brooke picked the one with carrots and other veggies. She needed to eat well. Unfortunately, the smell of the food heating in the microwave made her stomach heave. She rushed outside and leaned against the house, breathing in the night air. No one had ever told her that morning sickness could last all day.

On a whim, she sent a text to Alexis…

Are you busy? Want to come over? I haven't seen you in ages…

Alexis's response was almost immediate.

Sounds great. Are your parents home?

Brooke grinned. Alexis was no more a fan of Simon and Margaret Goodman than Austin was. She typed a single-word reply and threw in a few happy-face emojis for good measure…

NO! 😊😊😊

Alexis replied quickly.

See you soon.

While Brooke cleaned up the kitchen and waited for her friend, she debated how much of the truth to share. She could trust Alexis with her secrets. She had no doubts about that. But she didn't want to feel disloyal to Austin. The confusion was a dilemma she hadn't expected.

Alexis arrived barely half an hour later. After the two women hugged, Brooke led the way into the comfy den. "You want something to drink?" she asked. "A glass of wine, maybe?"

The other woman plopped down on the sofa with a sigh. "What are you having?"

Brooke felt her cheeks get hot. "Just water. Trying to be healthier. You know."

"Yeah. Probably a good idea. This whole bachelor auction may turn me into a raving alcoholic before it's over anyway."

Brooke curled up in an adjoining chair. "How are things going?"

Alexis shrugged. "I suppose you could say we're on schedule. Still, I'm putting out new fires every day. I can't imagine why there are people who *want* to do event planning for a living."

Brooke laughed, but she sympathized with her friend's frustration. Gus Slade, Alexis's grandfather, had insisted his granddaughter be in charge of the bachelor auction. No one ever said no to Gus, least of all his beleaguered family members.

Alexis was similar in height and build to Brooke, though Alexis was a bit taller, and her eyes were blue, not gray. The two women had been friends since childhood. Alexis was the same age as Brooke, but unlike Brooke, Alexis had been sent away to school at a young age and had developed a sophistication and confidence Brooke wondered if she herself would ever match.

Brooke studied the lines of exhaustion on her friend's face. "Sounds like you need a break. Have you seen Daniel lately?"

"No," Alexis said sharply. "Daniel and I are history. End of story."

"Sorry for bringing him up," Brooke muttered.

"No, I'm sorry," Alexis said quickly. Her guilty smile was apologetic. "But let's talk about you."

"Okay." Brooke paused, struggling for words. There really was no way to dance around the subject. "I'm pregnant."

Alexis's jaw dropped. She sat up straight and stared. "You're joking."

"No." Brooke shook her head.

"But who?" Her friend was understandably bewildered.

"Austin Bradshaw. The architect your grandfather hired to design and oversee the new club addition."

"I've run into him. Briefly." Alexis frowned. "He only arrived two weeks ago. Maybe not even that long."

"We met in Joplin just before Labor Day. It was never

supposed to be anything more than a…" The words stuck in her throat.

"A one-night stand?" Alexis winced.

"Yes. The pregnancy was an accident."

"Are you okay, Brookie?"

The childhood nickname suddenly made Brooke want to bawl, but at the same time, it was comforting in an odd way. This woman had known her forever. They had been through a lot.

"I've been sick. It's not fun, I'll tell you that. But I've decided I want the baby. I really do. Before we found out about the pregnancy, I was trying to talk Austin into a temporary marriage, so I could get my inheritance." Alexis knew all about the money from Brooke's grandmother and how her parents were refusing to let her open an art school.

"Do you think you can trust this man? He's practically a stranger. I don't like the idea of him having a shot at all those millions."

Brooke frowned. Alexis's concern made perfect sense, but she felt the need to defend her husband-to-be. "Austin is a decent, wonderful person. I have no worries on that score at all. In fact, he was the one who insisted on a prenup. He doesn't want people thinking he's a fortune hunter."

"Maybe he's just saying that to win your trust."

"He's not like that. He's a widower who loved his wife."

Alexis snorted. "And widowers can't be villains?"

"He's not a villain. He's a great guy."

"But he knocked you up, so there's that."

"It was an accident," Brooke said. "Neither of us did anything wrong. It just happened."

"Are you in love with him?" Alexis asked.

"No. We hardly know each other."

"Then why are you blushing?"

"I *could* love him, I think," Brooke said. "But he's still hung up on his dead wife." She released a heavy sigh. "They were college sweethearts. I can't compete with that. Besides, Austin has told me flat out that he's not interested in a relationship."

"Was that before or after you found out about the baby?"

Brooke gaped, trying to remember. "It doesn't matter. We've been very careful to talk about everything as *short-term*. I'll admit that the baby complicates things."

"I've got a bad feeling about this, Brooke. I understand why you need to get married. But this can't be a paper commitment only...not with the baby. You and Austin are going to be inextricably involved, indefinitely. Life will be messy. Particularly if you fall in love with him."

Having all her doubts spoken aloud was sobering. "I hear what you're saying... I do. But I have to make the best of a difficult situation. Austin has offered to support me until the inheritance comes through the courts. He's renting a house for the three of us."

Alexis arched a brow. "He's being awfully accommodating for a guy who buried his heart with his dead wife."

"Don't be like that."

"Like what?" Alexis's cynical smile was disturbing.

"I want the fairy-tale romance," Brooke cried. "Don't you think I do? When you and Daniel tried to run away as teenagers and then everything went south, I ached for you. And then all these years later you reconnected. Of *course* I want a love like that. But not everyone gets that chance. I have to make do with what I have."

Alexis stood and prowled, her expression tight. "You can forget about Daniel and me. Nothing has changed even though we're back in the same town. Ours was no grand love affair, believe me. All the reasons we couldn't make it work as teenagers are still there." She thumped her fist on the mantel. "I told you I don't want to talk about Daniel." She wiped her face, though Brooke hadn't realized until then that Alexis had been crying. "When is the wedding?" she asked.

Brooke pulled her knees to her chest. "I don't know," she said glumly. "We'll go the courthouse, I suppose. In Joplin, maybe. Not here."

"Do you want me to be there with you?"

Brooke nodded, her throat tight. "I'd like that."

"Okay, then." Alexis sighed, visibly shaking off her mood. "What can I do to help tonight?"

"Well," Brooke said, "I have two large suitcases and four boxes upstairs ready to be packed. I wouldn't mind a hand with that."

"Only two suitcases?"

"None of my clothes are going to fit…remember? I'll get the other stuff later. When my parents have had a chance to get used to the idea of me being gone."

"And being pregnant. And being married."

"You're not making me feel better."

"Sorry." On the way up to Brooke's room, Alexis ran her hand along the banister. "I wonder how many nights I spent in this house over the years."

"Who knows? But it was certainly a lot. I think my parents liked having you here, because you were a Slade and thus a good influence on me."

"Not after I tried to run off with the help and got banished for my indiscretions." The bitterness in her voice was impossible to miss.

Brooke paused on the top step and turned, looking down at Alexis. "I'm really sorry. This stupid town puts far too much emphasis on social standing. My mother actually called Austin a *handyman*. As if that was the worst insult she could come up with at the moment."

They walked down the hall and into Brooke's child-hood bedroom. The toys and school trophies had long since been packed away. The room had been professionally redecorated and painted. But Disney posters still hung inside her walk-in closet. At one time, Brooke had considered becoming a graphic artist. She loved color and design.

Alexis flopped down on the bed and stretched her arms over her head. "I feel like I should throw you a party. After all this time, you're finally escaping your parents' clutches."

"I love my mom and dad."

"I know you do, darlin', and that's why I love *you*. Despite the way they've treated you, you won't turn your back on them. Not everyone is as forgiving as you are."

Brooke gave her friend a pointed look. "Don't make

me out to be a saint. I'm not inviting them to the wedding. In fact, I'm not even telling them when it is. My mother would probably call in a mock bomb threat to the courthouse."

"Or she'd have your father fake a heart attack."

They dissolved into laughter, and the conversation moved onto lighter topics. In an hour, the packing was done.

Alexis studied the partially denuded bedroom. "Do you want to come to my place tonight? I hate to think of you staying here all by yourself."

"I appreciate the offer. But honestly, I need some time to think. To make sure I'm doing the right thing."

"It sounds like you've already made up your mind."

There was no criticism in Alexis's statement...only quiet concern.

Brooke shrugged. "I guess I have. I like Austin. He's willing to help me get my inheritance. He's interested in supporting his child, and he wants to play a role in the baby's future."

"What about you, Brooke? What do you want?"

"I'm not entirely sure. But I'll figure it out soon. I'm running out of time."

Austin drove to Joplin on Saturday. He didn't have to. There sure as hell was plenty going on at the club that needed his attention. But he had learned—when Jenny was ill—there was more to life than work.

His sister was thrilled to see him. A pot of his favorite chili bubbled on the stove, and she had gone the extra mile to make chocolate chip cookies. He shrugged out of his light jacket and hung it on the hook by the back door. "Hey, sis. Smells great in here."

Audra hugged him. "It's a sad day when I have to bribe you to get a visit."

Not for the world would he ever tell her this house held too many painful memories. Jenny had died in the bedroom just down the hall. Six years had passed. The raw grief had healed. Still, the house was not comfortable to him. Perhaps it never would be.

They had lunch together, talking, laughing, catching up. Audra was almost six years older than he was. In many ways she had been a second mother to him. She had been married briefly when he was in high school. But apparently the guy was a jackass, because the relationship ended after eighteen months. Audra never spoke of it, and she never dated seriously since.

Come to think of it, she and Austin had a lot in common. Too much pain in their pasts. Too little inclination to try again.

He knew that sooner or later she would grill him because of the phone call he had made to her the day he discovered Brooke was pregnant. She waited until he was on his second cup of coffee and his third cookie.

"So," she said, leaning her chair back on two legs and looking at him over the rim of her pink earthenware mug with the huge daisy painted on the side. "You want to tell me what's going on?"

He sighed inwardly. "Brooke's pregnant."

"The cute blonde from the bar?"

"Yep."

"Did she set you up?" Audra's suspicious frown had *mother hen* written all over it.

"Stand down, sis. This was entirely an accident. I won't go into details, but the kid is mine."

"What now?"

He told her about Brooke's inheritance and her dream of opening an art school and her crazy-ass parents. "I've rented a condo as of Monday. And I've offered to marry Brooke so she can get her money. Temporarily only."

Audra scowled. "You are so full of crap."

"Hey…" He held up his hands. "Why the attitude? I'm the good guy in this scenario."

"Are you planning on sleeping with her?"

"The condo has three bedrooms."

"That's not an answer and you know it. Tread carefully, Austin."

His neck got hot. "I don't follow."

She leaned forward and rested her elbows on the table. "I love you, little brother. But you're not the same man you were before Jenny got sick. When you were younger, you were the life of the party, always joking and laughing. After she died, you changed. I miss that old Austin. Honestly, though, I doubt if he's ever coming back."

His stomach curled. Nothing she had said was news to him. "What's your point?"

"Don't hurt this girl."

"I don't plan to hurt anyone."

"But that's the problem, kiddo. You think everything can stay light and easy. But you're not able to see this from a young woman's perspective, especially the one

I remember from the bar. She still had stars in her eyes, Austin. I'll bet when she looks at you, her heart races and she starts imagining a future where the two of you grow old together."

"That's where you're wrong," he said defensively. "I've been very clear about that. I told her I don't want another relationship."

Audra's visible skepticism underscored his own doubts. But what could he do? The course was set. He and Brooke were getting married.

Twelve

While Austin was busy with his own agenda Saturday morning, Brooke sat in her car in front of Natalie Valentine's bridal shop and tried to think of a cover story that wouldn't sound too unbelievable. Her phone said it was 9:57. The store opened at ten.

After Alexis left last night, Brooke had spent an hour wandering from room to room of her family home, wondering if she was jumping from the proverbial frying pan into the fire. How could she marry a man she barely knew?

On the other hand, how could she not?

She had eventually slept from midnight until seven and then spent an hour in the bathroom that morning retching miserably. This pregnancy thing was taking a toll on her body already. Her weight was down five pounds.

When she saw the hanging placard in the glass doorway flip from *Closed* to *Open*, she climbed out of the car and marched inside.

Natalie greeted her with a smile. "Hi, Brooke. You're out early. Can I help you find a dress for the auction? I assume that's why you're here. I've sold ten gowns in the last week already. If my business is any indicator, the charity bachelor gig is going to be a huge success."

"I'll just browse for a bit if that's okay," Brooke said, avoiding the question.

"Of course. Make yourself at home. There's coffee in the next room if you get thirsty."

When Natalie moved to greet another customer, Brooke breathed a sigh of relief. She wasn't prepared to explain why she needed a dress. The traditional wedding gowns in the back half of the salon beckoned with their satin and lace and bridal splendor, but she wouldn't let her wistful imagination go there. Reality was her currency. She had plans to make and a future to plot out.

She tried on six dresses before she found one that didn't make her feel self-conscious. The winning number was an ivory silk affair, strapless, nipped in at the waist, ending just below the knee. It was sophisticated, elegant and bridal enough for an informal courthouse wedding.

With the dress draped over her arm, she bumped open the fitting room door with her hip and nearly ran into Tessa Noble. The curvy African American woman with the sweet smile greeted Brooke warmly. "Hey,

Brooke. I haven't seen you in forever. Are you shopping for a charity auction dress...like me?"

Brooke hugged the other woman. "*You're* going? Tripp, too?" Tessa's brother was as popular as his sister, though Tripp was an extrovert, and Tessa definitely preferred staying out of the limelight.

Tessa chuckled. "Would you believe that Ryan Bateman has talked Tripp into being one of the bachelors?"

"Oh, wow. Your brother is a hunk. The bidding will go wild."

Tessa rolled her eyes. "Yeah. That's what I think. He'll eat it up. But it's all for a good cause."

"So what kind of dress do you want? I bet you would look amazing in hot pink. Or scarlet maybe. Even emerald green."

Tessa chewed her bottom lip. "Oh, I don't know, Brooke. I was thinking something a little less flashy."

"I can understand that. But every woman deserves to look her best. Do you mind if I hang around and see what you try on?" She sensed that Tessa might need a gentle push in the right direction.

"Of course not. Is that what you're going to wear?"

Brooke felt her face get hot. "Maybe. I have a couple of other occasions coming up during the holidays, so I wanted to be prepared. Here," she said, pulling two outfits off the rack when she saw what size Tessa was eyeing. "Humor me." The red or the fuchsia—either choice would be sensational.

Tessa seemed dubious. "I'd prefer something with a little less wattage. This one might work." She held out an unexceptional gown that was perfectly plain.

Brooke wrinkled her nose. "Basic black is acceptable for a formal occasion, of course, but you have a majestic figure, Tessa. Play to your strengths. Don't hide in the shadows."

"I'm not hiding," Tessa insisted. "I love my body. Or at least as much as any woman does." She grinned. "But that doesn't mean I want everyone gawking at it."

"Isn't there something in between? Then again, my life isn't exactly going according to plan lately, so who am I to hand out advice?" Brooke admitted the truth ruefully.

Natalie had apparently been watching the good-natured standoff. She joined them and gave Tessa a reassuring smile. "You're not the first woman to be nervous about stepping out of your comfort zone. Here's an idea. Take all three possibilities home overnight, plus another one or two if you like. Try them on in the comfort of your own bedroom with your own shoes and jewelry. Keep the tags attached, of course. I think—under those circumstances—you'll end up with exactly the right outfit for the occasion."

While Tessa took her time selecting from a wide array of choices, Brooke said her goodbyes and followed Natalie back to the cash register to pay for her purchases. Natalie took Brooke's credit card, then slid the dress into a clear garment bag. "This one is lovely. You can dress it up or down so many ways. And if it's a cooler evening, some kind of golden, gauzy shawl would be pretty."

Brooke nodded. "Yes." She was almost tongue-tied. It had never been her intention to hide her pregnancy forever. But now it seemed difficult to dump the news on people without divulging far more than she wanted to about her personal life.

By the time she made it back to her car and spread the dress bag out in the trunk, she was starving. She still had two stops to make, but they would have to wait. Instead, she drove the short distance to the diner and grabbed chicken noodle soup and a chicken pita sandwich to go.

It wasn't the easiest meal to eat in the car, but she didn't want to run into anyone she knew. How was she going to explain Austin to the world? How was she going to explain her pregnancy? The deeper she got into the chaotic whirl of events she herself had set in motion with one crazy night in Joplin, the more out of control she felt.

Babies were amazing and wonderful. She truly believed that. But this little one was turning Brooke's world upside down and backward in a big way.

She parked beside the courthouse and ate her lunch slowly, huddling in her navy wool sweater and wishing she had dressed more warmly for the day. The weather, as predicted, had taken a nasty turn. The skies were dull and gray. The temperature had dropped at least fifteen degrees. A steady, driving rain stripped any remaining leaves from the trees. Fall, her favorite season, would soon turn to winter.

Royal's winters were mild, for the most part. Still, it was a good thing she had finished the outdoor murals. She couldn't risk getting sick. Not with so much at stake.

What was Austin doing right now? Was he at the club? Working on the new addition? It pained her that she had no idea.

When she couldn't put it off any longer, she got out and locked the car. The wind made her umbrella virtually useless. The lawyer her parents used occupied an office in the annex across the street from the courthouse. Brooke had an appointment.

The dour older gentleman took her back to his overly formal suite right on time. He didn't seem happy to see her, particularly after a tense fifteen-minute conversation. "So you see," Brooke said, "I'll need the prenup right away. And I'll need your assurance that what we've discussed doesn't leave this room. I know my mother tries to twist people to her way of thinking, but you are obligated to keep my confidence. Right? I've told her I'm getting married. I just haven't said when."

The lawyer blustered a bit, pretending to be insulted, but Brooke knew there was a better than even chance he would dial her mother's cell number as soon as Brooke walked out of the room.

The man scowled. "Your parents are looking out for your best interests, Miss Goodman."

"It's *Ms.*," she said. "I'm twenty-six years old. Plenty old enough to know my own mind. I'll bring you the marriage license as soon as I have it. And then?"

He shrugged. "I'll file the paperwork. Barring any kind of hiccups, the transfer of your grandmother's assets should be fairly straightforward."

"What kind of hiccups?" Brooke asked, mildly alarmed.

"Merely a figure of speech."

She left the office soon after. This time the queasiness in her stomach had nothing to do with her pregnancy. Surely her parents wouldn't try to contest her grandmother's will. It was ironclad. Wasn't it?

Unfortunately, the meeting with the lawyer directly preceded her first visit with the ob-gyn who would be caring for Brooke during her pregnancy and birth. The woman frowned when she saw Brooke's blood pressure. "Have you had issues with your BP in the past, Ms. Goodman?"

Brooke flushed. "No, ma'am. I had kind of an upsetting afternoon. That's all. I'll be fine."

The appointment lasted almost an hour. Brooke was poked and prodded and examined from head to toe. Except for the blood pressure thing, she was in perfect health. The doctor gave her a stern lecture about stress and demonstrated a few relaxation techniques. At the very last, Brooke received the piece of information she had been waiting for.

The doctor smiled. "Since you seem to know the exact date you conceived, it makes things easier. I've marked your due date as May 14. Congratulations, Ms. Goodman. I'll see you in another month."

Brooke took her paperwork, handed over the copay and walked out of the office on unsteady legs. Deep down, perhaps she had been hoping that the whole pregnancy thing was a mistake. Except for the nausea and occasional light-headedness, she still didn't *feel* pregnant.

But now, there was no doubt.

She stopped at the pharmacy to pick up her new vitamins—tablets the size of horse pills—and then she drove by the piece of property she hoped to buy soon. The empty lot sat forlorn. Brooke leaned her arms on the steering wheel and stared through the rain-spattered windshield.

Her art center would be the kind of place where she could bring her infant to work. Being her own boss would be the best of both worlds. She could be a parent and still create her dream of a thriving studio for children and young teens to pursue their artistic endeavors.

She wished she had brought Austin here. He needed to see what he was helping her accomplish. And besides, she missed him. Her body yearned for his in a way that was physical and real and impossible to ignore. Already, her life seemed empty when he wasn't around.

That thought should have alarmed her, but she was too tired to wrestle with the ramifications of falling for the handsome cowboy. She would try to protect her heart. It was all she could do.

When she returned home, it was as if her wistful thoughts had conjured a man out of thin air. Austin was sitting on the front porch when she walked up the path. Her parents had given the house staff the week-end off, not out of any sense of altruism but because they didn't want to pay hourly employees when they were out of town.

Hence, there had been no one to answer the door.

Austin unfolded his lean, lanky body and stretched. "I was beginning to think you weren't coming back."

"I live here," she pointed out calmly, trying not to

let him see that her palms were sweaty and her heart was beating far too fast.

He grinned. "Not for long." He dropped a kiss on her forehead. "I have a surprise for you. Will you come with me? No questions asked?"

She hadn't been looking forward to an evening all alone. "Yes. Do I need to change?"

"Nope." He steered her back down the walk in the direction she had come moments before. Her wedding dress was still in the trunk of her car, so she used her keys to beep the lock. It would be fine for the moment. Before she could climb into the cab of the truck, Austin put his hands at her waist, lifted her and set her gently on the seat.

She wanted to make a joke about how strong he was and that he was her prince charming, but she stopped herself. This wasn't an ordinary flirtation. They weren't an ordinary couple.

Once they began driving, it didn't take long for her to realize that Austin was taking her to their new condo. When he parked at the curb, she shot him a teasing glance. "Breaking and entering? Not really my style."

Austin reached in his pocket and dangled a set of keys in front of her face. "I sweet-talked the rental agent into the giving me the keys early. She made me swear we wouldn't move in until Monday. Insurance regulations, you know. But tonight, it's all ours."

On the top step sat a jaunty pumpkin. His jack-o'-lantern face had been carved into a perpetual glare.

Brooke laughed softly. "You did this?"

Austin nodded. "Yes."

"I love it." Warmth seeped into her soul. That and the reassurance that she wasn't being entirely foolish. All her doubts settled for the moment, lost in the excitement of being with Austin. "Did you mention dinner? I seem to be perpetually hungry these days."

"Follow me." He unlocked the front door with a flourish. In the living room, he had somehow managed to procure a romantic meal, complete with candles and strawberries and a crystal vase filled with daisies. "You've had a lot of stress lately, darlin'. I thought we both deserved a break."

She looked up at him through damp eyes. "A lovely idea. Thank you, Austin."

He cocked his head, a slight frown appearing between his eyebrows. "Something's wrong."

Brooke sat down on the floor and leaned back against the sofa, stretching out her legs. "Not really. Just a lot of *adulting* today."

"Like what?" he asked, joining her.

"Well, the lawyer's office, for one."

His gaze sharpened. "The prenup?"

"Yes."

"Good."

"And I got a dress for our wedding."

"Excellent."

"And I also had my first visit with my ob-gyn."

His lips twitched. "I'm impressed."

"No, you're not," she said slowly. "You're making fun of me."

"I'm not, I swear. You're a list maker, aren't you?"

"To the bone. Is that a bad thing?"

He leaned over and kissed the side of her neck, sending shivers down her spine. "I like a woman who can focus."

She moaned when he pulled her close and found her mouth with his. His lips were warm and firm and masculine. Arching her neck, she leaned into him and, for a few exciting moments, let herself indulge in the magic that was Austin.

But when the kiss threatened to burn out of control, she pulled back, still hesitant, still unsure of the big picture, no matter how much she craved his touch.

She cleared her throat. "Will I seem needy if I say I missed you today?"

"I missed you, too, Brooke." His smile was lopsided, almost rueful. "In fact, I should have taken you with me, I think."

"Taken me where?"

He hesitated briefly before responding. "I went to see my sister, Audra."

"The tall redhead?"

"The one and only."

"Was it a friendly, low-key visit, or an I'm-about-to-get-married announcement?" she asked.

He scraped his hands through his hair. "The second one. Audra thinks I'm making a big mistake."

"Oh." Brooke's stomach curled into a tight knot of hurt and embarrassment. "She's probably right."

"Audra didn't have all the facts. I filled her in. And of course, the baby was the tipping point."

"Oh, goody. She's probably out right now getting my sister-in-law-of-the-year T-shirt."

"You're getting cranky," he said. "Eat a taco."

Austin must have had help with this picnic, because the food was still warm. Even so, her stomach revolted. She took one bite and set the plate aside. "Alexis thinks we're making a big mistake, too."

"Alexis Slade? Gus's granddaughter?"

"I told you she's my friend. She gave me the mural job, remember?"

He nodded. "I do. What's her beef with me?"

"It's not you," Brooke said. She rested her chin on her knees. "She thinks I'll let my gratitude for what you're doing cause me to confuse sexual attraction with love."

He went still, his entire body frozen for a full three seconds. At last he sighed, almost silently. "But you told her we've been very clear about our expectations... right?"

"I told her."

"Then what's the problem?"

The problem was that Austin Bradshaw was a gorgeous, sexy, intensely masculine man who also happened to be a decent, hardworking, kind human being. A platonic relationship might have worked if Brooke had thought of him as a brother. But from the first moment she'd set eyes on him in that bar in Joplin, she had wanted him. Badly.

Wanting was a short step to needing. And needing segued into loving with no trouble at all.

She managed a smile. "We don't have a problem. I think everything is going exactly according to plan."

Thirteen

In hindsight, Austin had to admit that preparing a romantic indoor picnic for a woman might be sending mixed signals. All he had wanted to do was reassure Brooke about moving in with him. To let her know that leaving her parents' house was the right thing to do.

But now she seemed skittish around him, especially after that kiss.

Making Brooke smile and laugh was rapidly becoming an obsession. The way her gray eyes lit up when she was happy. The excitement in her voice when she told him about her plans. Even her shy anticipation about having a baby she had never meant to conceive at all.

Perhaps he was the one in danger.

He filled his plate in hopes that Brooke would follow suit. She had been so very sick these last few days, she was losing weight already. Her petite frame didn't have pounds to spare. Right now, her cheekbones were far too pronounced—her collarbone, too.

She carried an air of exhaustion, though he had a hunch her fatigue was as much emotional as it was physical. Hearing and seeing what her parents had put her through in recent months made him angry on her behalf.

Out of the corner of his eye, he saw her take a bite of the savory shredded-pork taco. Soon, she finished the entire thing, including most of the brown rice alongside it.

"Another one?" he asked.

Brooke eyed the platter longingly. "I don't know. I don't want to push it. The food is amazing, though. Where did you get it?"

"One of my carpenters is from Mexico. He and his family just opened a new restaurant on the south side of town. I told him what I was doing tonight, and he helped me get everything together."

"Give that man a raise." She put a hand on her stomach and grimaced. "I'll wait fifteen minutes, and if everything stays down, I'm going to have a second." She wiped a dollop of sour cream from the edge of her mouth, eyeing him with an expression he couldn't decipher. "I've been thinking," she said slowly.

"About what?" He dunked a chip in cheese sauce and ate it.

"Marriage. My art studio. Us."

His gut tightened. "I thought we settled all that."

"Well, when the two most important people in our lives wave red flags, it *should* make us think twice."

"Our business is our business, Brooke. Neither of them understand where we stand on this."

"At least hear me out. You don't want to be married again. And you don't want to have a child. I can't do anything about that second part, but I did think of a way we could skip walking down the aisle."

He stood up and folded his arms across his chest. "Oh?"

"The terms of Grammy's will state that I get the money when I marry or on my thirtieth birthday. I'll hit that mark three years and two months from now. Instead of marrying me, you *could* simply cosign the loan for my art studio with me. Then my parents wouldn't try to contest the will or stop the wedding. You wouldn't be legally tied to a woman who isn't Jenny. And I wouldn't have to feel guilty for ruining your life."

Austin stared at her, feeling shifting sand beneath his feet. Everything she said made sense. Yet he hated every word. "Come here, woman." He reached down, grabbed her hand and drew her to her feet. He put his hands on her face, cupping her cheeks in his palms. "No one," he said firmly, "makes me do something I don't want to do. I'm not marrying you because I *have* to. I don't feel trapped. You're not taking advantage of my good nature."

Her eyes widened. "I'm not?"

He dragged her against him, letting her feel the full extent of his arousal. His erection throbbed between them, pressing into her soft belly, telegraphing his intent. "This marriage is convenient for me, too," he drawled. "I want you in my bed every night. I want you in a million different ways. I want to take you over and over again and make you cry out my name until neither of us can remember to breathe. You're a fire in my blood."

He paused, his chest heaving. The words had poured out of him like hot lava, churning to the surface without warning.

Brooke stared at him, eyes wide, lips parted. He put a hand on her flat belly. "This baby is *ours*," he said softly. "Yours and mine. I never had that with Jenny. So that makes you pretty damned rare and unique. I don't have it in me to love again. I won't lie about that. But I'll be good to you, Brooke. Can't that be enough?"

Her lower lip wobbled. "I suppose." Dampness sheened her eyes. He could fall into those deep gray pools and never come up for air. For six long years he had wandered in a wasteland of despair and pain. Every part of his soul was awakening now. The rebirth hurt in a different kind of way, which was why he had put safeguards in place.

This thing with Brooke was special, but he wouldn't let it drag him under.

He scooped her into his arms and walked toward the master bedroom. The house had been staged for showing. Only a bedspread covered the mattress. Austin didn't care. It had been too long since he'd been intimate with Brooke and felt her soft body strain against his.

Brooke was silent. For once, he couldn't tell what she was thinking. He laid her down and lowered himself beside her, settling onto his right hip and propping his head on his hand. "I didn't ask," he said slowly, suddenly unsure of the situation. "I want to make love to you. Is that okay?"

She chewed her lip. "Have sex, you mean?"

"Don't do that."

"Do what?"

"Pick at words. You know what I mean."

She laughed softly, though he was convinced he saw doubts in her eyes. "I do know what you mean," she said. "And yes. I want to have sex."

He winced inwardly at her insistence on the more clinical phrase. Was she trying to make a point, or was the *L* word as much a problem for her as it was for him?

Shaking off the worrisome thoughts, he unbuttoned her designer jeans and placed a hand flat on her belly. "This is the first time we've done this knowing that you're…" The word stuck in his throat. With some consternation, it occurred to him that he had *never* made love to a woman who was growing another human.

Brooke grinned. "Pregnant? Is that the word you're looking for? All the parts still work the same. The doctor said I have no restrictions in that area. And the good news is… I can't get pregnant *again*."

"Very funny."

He leaned over and kissed her taut stomach. "You have a cute navel, Ms. Goodman. I can't wait to see it grow."

"I'll have to finish the day-care murals soon before I get too fat to climb up a ladder."

"Not fat," he muttered, reaching underneath her to unfasten her bra. "Rounded. Voluptuous. Gorgeous."

Brooke giggled until he took one nipple in his mouth

and suckled it. Her tiny cry of pleasure sank claws of hunger into his gut. She tasted like temptation and sin, a heady cocktail.

"Tell me you want this."

"I already did."

"Beg me…"

The gruff demand showed Brooke a side of her cowboy she had never experienced before tonight. He wasn't above torturing her. The rough slide of his tongue across her sensitive flesh was exquisite.

She cradled his head in her hands, sliding her fingers into his silky hair and pulling him closer. "Please," she whispered. "Please, please, please make love to me, Austin."

"I thought you'd never ask."

He undressed her slowly. The house was warm. Even so, the erotic pace covered her body in gooseflesh. Austin's hooded gaze and flushed cheekbones signaled a man on the edge.

In the silence, his ragged breathing was unsteady. Brooke, on the other hand, wasn't sure she was breathing at all.

She hadn't expected this time with Austin to be any different. But the baby was changing things already. This tiny life growing inside her had seemed like an ephemeral idea…a hard-to-believe notion.

Here…now, though, the child was almost tangible. She and Austin had created something magical. Was it her imagination, or was the tenderness in his gaze more pronounced tonight? Despite the unmistakable hunger in his touch, he had reined in his need. He was handling her like spun glass.

Unbuttoning his shirt was the next logical step. It was easier now to touch him, easier than it had been the first time, or even the second. She was beginning to know what he liked, what brushes of her fingertips made him groan.

He had undressed her down to her bikini underwear. She straddled him and leaned forward to stroke the planes of his chest. His skin was hot. The place where his heart thudded beneath her fingertips beckoned. She kissed him there, lingering to absorb his strength, his wildly beating life force.

"I won't regret this," she whispered. "I won't regret *you*." She hoped it was a vow she could keep.

Austin lifted her aside and rolled to his feet…just long enough to strip off his remaining clothes. He was magnificent in his nudity. Not even the scar on his left thigh from a childhood injury could detract from his power and virile beauty.

He came back to her, scooted her up in the bed and settled between her thighs. "I can't wait," he growled. He took her in one forceful thrust, stealing her breath. The connection was electric, the moment cataclysmic.

For a panicked instant, Brooke saw the folly of her plan. Doggedly, she shoved the painful vision aside. She had Austin in this moment. Nothing could ruin that.

The condo faded away. Not even the smell of fresh paint nor the faint sounds of laughter and traffic on the street outside could impinge on her consciousness.

Nothing existed but the feel of Austin's big, warm body loving hers.

Emotion rose in her chest, hectic and sweet. She wanted to call out his name, to tell him how much he gave her, how much she wanted still.

But she bit her tongue. She kept silent. She would not offer what he did not want or need.

Perhaps pregnancy made her body more receptive, more attuned to the give and take between them. She felt as if she had climbed inside his skin…as though the air in his lungs was hers and the beat of her heart was his.

They moved together slowly, all urgency gone. It was as if they had been lovers for a hundred years. Because despite the differences that kept them apart, she knew him. *Intimately.* And in that moment, she fell all the way into the deep. She loved Austin Bradshaw.

The knowledge was neither sweet nor comforting. It was a raw, jagged blade that ripped at her serenity, severing her hope for the future.

Her arms tightened around his neck. "Don't stop," she groaned. "Please don't stop." She concentrated on the physical bliss, shoving aside all else that would have to be dealt with later.

This was Austin, her Austin. And she loved him.

Her climax was explosive and deeply satisfying. Austin groaned and found his release. Seconds later, he reached for a corner of the bedspread and pulled it over their naked bodies. Rolling onto his back, he tucked her against his right side. In moments, she heard the gentle sound of his breathing as he slid into sleep.

Presumably he had been up early for the drive to Joplin. Chances were, he had gone by the club to check on his big project before arranging this surprise. The man worked hard.

His left hand rested flat on his chest. She lifted it and played with his fingers, twining hers with his. Then she saw something that somehow she had never noticed before—perhaps because it was the kind of thing a person could only see if they were staring closely.

On the third finger of Austin's left hand, there was a white indentation where his wedding ring had resided. The sight shocked her. She rubbed the shallow groove. Austin never moved. His hand was lax in hers, trusting.

Pain like she had never known strangled her. She swallowed a moan. The night she had met him was the first time he had been without that ring. She had coaxed him into bed that night. Or maybe he had coaxed her. The lines were fuzzy. If they were to marry this week, would he be expecting a wedding band from Brooke?

She couldn't do it. She couldn't replace a man's devotion to the love of his life with an empty symbol of a convenient union.

Stricken and confused, she climbed out of bed and dressed. Ironically, despite her emotional upheaval, her stomach now cooperated and announced its displeasure by growling loudly.

The sparsely outfitted kitchen did have a microwave. She fixed a plate of leftover food, nuked it and sat at the table.

Austin found her minutes later. He had dressed, but his shirt was still unbuttoned, giving her glimpses of his hard chest. He yawned and dropped a kiss on top of her head. "Sorry. I've had a few late nights recently. This project is one snag after the other."

She murmured something noncommittal.

He grabbed seconds for himself as well and joined her. "You okay, honey?"

"Yes." It was a humongous lie, but under the circumstances, perhaps the Almighty would forgive her.

Austin wiped his mouth. "I don't see any point in postponing our wedding. Does Wednesday work for you? I thought I'd tell my crew I have personal business that day. I happen to know that Audra is free. Do you think Alexis can join us?"

Brooke's throat was so tight it was difficult to speak. "I'll ask her. But I'm sure her schedule is flexible."

He frowned, staring off into space. "I know there will be gossip. Can't be helped. People will wonder why we're not taking a honeymoon. We'll simply say that the club-addition project is under a tight deadline so we're waiting until after Thanksgiving."

"That makes sense."

"What about your parents? I don't want you to have regrets, Brooke."

Too late for that. Hysteria bubbled in her throat. "The old me would have invited them. Even knowing what I know, I would have invited them because it's the proper thing to do. But they don't want to come, and even worse, they would almost definitely give us grief."

"Your brothers?"

She shook her head. "They won't have any interest in this, believe me. Alexis is all I need."

"Okay, then." He reached across the table and took her hand. "What kind of flowers do you like? I want you to have a bouquet." His gaze was open, warm… nothing at all to suggest that this wedding ceremony—modest though it was to be—might bring back memories of another, happier day.

"That's not necessary."

He squeezed her fingers, his smile teasing and intimate. "You'll be my bride, Brooke. Despite the circumstances, that's a fact. If you don't tell me, I'll get something atrociously gaudy, like purple carnations."

She laughed in spite of herself. "Oh, heck, no. Make it white roses." She paused. "And maybe white heather." Once upon a time she had researched flower meanings for an art project in college. White heather symbolized protection and a promise that wishes do come true. If any of that nonsense were real, she needed all the good karma and mojo she could summon.

"I'll do my best," he said.

They gathered up the remains of the dinner. Darkness had fallen.

"We should go," Brooke muttered. "I have a few more things to pack." She didn't really want to leave, but the longer she stayed, the more she felt the pull of that bed and this man and those impossible dreams.

"How 'bout I come with you now and load up the boxes you already have finished?"

"You wouldn't rather do that tomorrow?"

"No. I plan to spend most of the day at the club. Since I'm missing work Wednesday, I want to get a jump on this week's schedule. Things are moving fast now."

They *were* moving fast…too fast. "That makes sense," she said.

"And what about you?"

"Me? Um…"

He grinned. "Sorry. Didn't know it was a hard question."

"Alexis and I usually go to early mass and then have brunch. But she's not available this Sunday. I thought I'd finish the last of my packing and then maybe call my parents. I won't be there when they get home Monday night. Might as well break the news to them now."

"That won't be pleasant." He sobered, his jaw tightening.

"No. But it has to be done."

He pulled her into his arms and held her close. "They should be proud of you, Brooke. I'm sorry your mom and dad haven't been there to support you. I wish things were different."

The painful irony of his statement mocked her. *I wish things were different.* So did she. A million times over. No matter how much she told herself she was making the best of a difficult situation, she couldn't escape the gut-clenching certainty that she was making the biggest mistake of her life.

Fourteen

Sunday felt like the equivalent of a condemned man's last meal. Tomorrow Brooke would move into a new home with Austin. Wednesday she would legally become his wife.

These last peaceful hours in her childhood house constituted one final chance to make a run for it…to change the course of her destiny. Had it not been for a broken condom and a forgotten birth-control pill, perhaps she would have done just that. Maybe she would have found other businesspeople in Royal besides Alexis who were willing to stand up to Margaret Goodman and give Brooke a job. Maybe Brooke could have then found a roommate and a simple, inexpensive apartment.

Maybe she could have been free.

Her dream of an art studio would have been majorly postponed, but that was the case with a lot of people's dreams. And then some just never came true.

Now she faced the prospect of being trapped in a loveless marriage with the one man she wanted more than life itself. Her body craved his lovemaking. She yearned for his smiles, his teasing touch. But she was very much afraid that she had no future with Austin. How could she compete with the memory of his dead wife?

She slept fitfully and woke up sick. The routine was becoming familiar to her now—lukewarm tea and plain crackers after she emptied her stomach. The doctor had told her the nausea might subside in another few weeks as she entered her second trimester. Then again, it might not.

Eventually, her energy returned, at least enough to finish cleaning out the last of her bedroom closets and bathroom drawers. Though the housekeeper would return tomorrow, Brooke did all the vacuuming anyway. By two o'clock, her presence in the Goodman mansion was virtually erased. All that remained were her toiletries and one small overnight case.

Because Austin had loaded her boxes and large suitcases into his truck last night, tomorrow morning would be almost anticlimactic. All she would have to do on her way to work would be to walk out and shut the door.

She was putting the vacuum away in the utility closet off the kitchen when she heard a commotion in the garage. Her heart jumped. The alarm beeped, signaling that someone had shut it off.

Moments later Brooke's parents walked into the kitchen.

She gaped at them, glanced at the calendar and frowned. "I thought you weren't coming back until tomorrow." Her stomach clenched. That last awful meal with her parents and Austin had been a dreadful experience. She didn't want a repeat. The one saving grace was that her mother's temper usually burned hot and quick, and then she moved on to her next victim.

Either that or her parents were biding their time, preparing for their next military offensive. Brooke would be on her guard, just in case.

Margaret Goodman waved a hand and dumped her purse and tote on the island, her expression harried. "Your father wasn't feeling well. We managed to book an earlier flight. I'm going to call Henrietta immediately and have her come fix dinner."

Brooke winced inwardly. Her mother was essentially helpless in the domestic arena. "I don't mind cooking for you, Mama. Something simple, anyway. Baked chicken? A nice salad?"

Her father's face brightened, but her mother was already shaking her head. "I pay for the privilege of having my staff on call. It's not like I'm dragging her out of bed at midnight. Henrietta won't mind at all."

Maybe she would and maybe she wouldn't. It was a moot point. When Margaret Goodman delivered an edict, everyone jumped.

Despite what Brooke had told Austin about making a phone call to her parents today, she changed her mind. She had been preparing herself mentally to come over at dinnertime tomorrow before going to the condo. She had concluded that the conversation was one she needed to have face-to-face. Now fate, or her father's indigestion, had offered a much quicker and easier solution.

But it also meant delaying the inevitable for several hours, a nerve-inducing span of time in which she rehearsed her speech a dozen times. She had to wait for her mother to take a shower and change out of her *nasty* travel clothes. The Goodmans always flew first-class, so it was hard to imagine how much nastiness there could be on Margaret's powder-blue Chanel pantsuit. Still…

And her father had to catch up on sporting events he had missed while he was gone. He holed up in his man cave immediately.

Brooke was left to hide out in her room with her laptop researching baby furniture online. It was a delightful pastime. Even so, it wasn't enough of a distraction to calm her nerves.

Too bad she couldn't be over at the new condo handing out candy to trick-or-treaters. That would be fun. The Goodman home was in a gated community where the houses were spread far apart. No little ghosts and goblins would be ringing the doorbell here tonight.

The minutes on the clock crept by. Henrietta arrived. Brooke saw the cook's car out her window. Soon afterward, appetizing smells began wafting upstairs. Dinner was almost invariably served at six thirty. Margaret's doctor had told her that eating too late would make her gain weight.

At last, the three Goodmans sat down together in the formal dining room, and the first course was served.

Brooke would have far preferred eating at the cozy kitchen table in the breakfast nook. Her mother, however, believed in keeping up appearances. Brooke's father didn't have a dog in the fight, but he had given up caring about such things years ago.

Because Brooke was uncomfortable talking about very personal subjects in front of staff, she waited until dessert was served. Fresh apple tarts with cream. The timing meant Henrietta would be in the kitchen for at least the next half hour cleaning up the dishes.

Brooke took a deep breath. "Mom, Dad... I wanted to let you know that I'm moving out tomorrow."

Her father never lifted his head. He continued to eat his dessert as if afraid someone was going to snatch it away from him. Since it was definitely not on his approved diet, perhaps that was a valid fear.

Margaret, however, swallowed a bite, took a sip of wine and sat back in her chair. "Where on earth would you go, Brooke? You haven't a dollar to your name."

"And whose fault is that, Mama? You've deliberately sabotaged every attempt I've made to be independent."

Her mother didn't deny the charge. "Perhaps I'm afraid of the empty-nest syndrome."

Brooke rolled her eyes. "Oh, please."

Her mother lifted a shoulder. "I'm told that's a *thing.*"

"Not for you. You're too busy conquering the world. And that's not bad," Brooke said quickly. "You've always set a good example for me as a woman who can do anything she sets her mind to..."

"I sense your compliment is wrapped around a piece of rotting fish."

Margaret Goodman had always been a drama queen, a larger-than-life figure. She ruled her world by the sheer force of her personality—along with fear and intimidation.

"The compliment is sincere, Mother. But I'm telling you it's time for me to find my own way in the world."

"With this *handyman*?"

"Austin is a highly trained architect. He's brilliant, in fact."

"He hasn't held down a job in over six years. Your father and I had him investigated."

Brooke swallowed her anger with difficulty. "He nursed his dying wife. He told you that."

Her father looked up. "People say a lot of things, Brooke. Don't be naive. We won't apologize for being concerned."

Margaret nodded. "Besides, the wife has been gone a long time."

"My God, Mama. Have some compassion. He loved her. I think he still does."

For once, a tinge of genuine concern flickered in her mother's expression. "Then why, in God's name, Brooke, are you so hell-bent on throwing in your lot with this cowboy? He'll break your heart. Tell her, Simon."

Brooke's father grimaced. "Your mother may sometimes be prone to overstating the facts, but in this instance, I happen to agree with her. The man got you pregnant, Brooke, fully aware that you're an heiress. It looks bad, baby. And I know you. You've got romance in your soul. You want the happily-ever-after. But this architect isn't it. Give it time, Brooke. Someone else will come along."

The fact that they weren't yelling was actually worse. To have her parents speak to her as an adult was such an anomaly she felt as if the universe had tilted. "I appreciate everything you both have done for me. And even now, I appreciate the fact that you want me to be happy. I do. But I have to stand on my own feet. I'm going to be a mother."

"You could put the baby up for adoption," Margaret said. "Privately. In Dallas. This will change your whole life, Brooke."

"Yes, Mama. You're right. I didn't want to get pregnant. I didn't plan to have a baby so soon. Still, that's where I am. Despite the circumstances, I do want this child. He or she will be the next in a new line of Goodmans. Doesn't that excite you even a little bit?"

Both of her parents stared at her. Her father's expression was conflicted. With Brooke gone, there would be no one around to deflect Margaret's crazy train.

Brooke's mother's seemed to age suddenly. "I've never seen you like this, Brooke. So calm. So grown-up."

"Well, Mom, it had to happen sometime. I don't want to fight with either of you. I love you. But I have new priorities now. If you can respect those, I think we'll all be happier."

Her father grimaced. "It's not too late to break things off with the Bradshaw man. If this art studio business is so important to you, I can fund that, whether or not your mother agrees."

"Simon!" Margaret's outrage turned her face crimson.

He gave his wife a truculent stare. "Well, I can." He shrugged sheepishly, coming around to hug Brooke before releasing her and pouring himself another scotch. "I've let your mother take the reins, but I won't stand by and see you heartbroken by a bad relationship. You're my baby girl."

Brooke was completely caught off guard. "Thank you, Daddy. That means the world to me. I'll keep your offer in mind."

Margaret Goodman stared at her daughter. "I hope you won't do anything to tarnish our standing in the community."

Brooke flinched. The chilly words were their own condemnation. "I understand your concern, Mother. I'll do my best."

Monday morning, Brooke didn't see either of her parents when she came downstairs. While she had been in her bathroom miserably ill, Margaret and Simon Goodman had left for work.

The much-dreaded confrontation was over. Brooke had faced her two-headed nemesis and won. Or so it seemed.

Shouldn't there be some kind of trophy for what happened last night? When an adult child navigated the chilly waters of independence, surely there needed to be some permanent marker. The feeling of anticlimax as she said goodbye to her childhood home and climbed into her car was disheartening.

She had been counting on an exciting day at the club

to boost her spirits. Fortunately, that was an understatement. While she was outdoors taking one last critical look at her garden murals, a crew showed up from a regional magazine to do a story about the bachelor auction and all the renovations.

The reporter interviewed Brooke. The photographer took dozens of shots. Alexis was escorting the duo.

While the two professionals conferred, Brooke pulled Alexis aside. "Any chance you're free to be my maid of honor on Wednesday morning?"

She'd been hoping Alexis would squeal with excitement. Unfortunately, nothing had changed. Her friend wrinkled her nose. "You realize I can't say no to you, Brookie. But I have strong reservations."

"Duly noted."

"What time?"

"I don't know. We'll probably leave for Joplin first thing. Austin and I will talk tonight."

"So you're really moving in with him?"

"I am."

Alexis gnawed her lower lip. "I wish I could talk you out of this. But I'm hardly in a position to hand out romantic advice. Just promise me you'll be careful."

"What does that even mean? The man is only trying to do right by me and his child. He's not some wacko ax murderer."

"I'm not worried about your physical safety. I'm afraid he'll break your heart."

I'm afraid he'll break your heart.

Alexis's words reverberated in Brooke's head for

the remainder of the day. Perhaps because they echoed Brooke's worst fears.

Could she keep her emotional distance? Was that even possible?

Austin met her on the front steps of the club just after five. They had texted back and forth during the afternoon, and his mood was upbeat.

When she stepped outside, he gave her a big grin. "I skipped lunch. What if I take you to dinner at La Maison? To celebrate?"

What exactly were they celebrating? She was afraid to ask.

Instead, she looked down at her black pants and cream sweater. "I'm not really dressed for that place." La Maison was one of Royal's premier dining establishments.

Austin waved a dismissive hand. "It's Monday night. Nobody will care."

Again, they left her car behind. The restaurant was in the opposite direction from the condo, so they could pick up the vehicle later.

Once they were seated at a table for two beside the window, Brooke felt herself relax. "This was a great idea," she said. "I didn't realize how stressful it was going to be to talk to my parents. They didn't go ballistic, but it wasn't easy."

Austin poured her a glass of sparkling water from the crystal carafe the waiter had left on their table. "You should be proud of yourself."

"I am," she said, sipping her water slowly and gazing absently at their fellow diners. It was true. Despite her current circumstances, she felt in control of her life. It was a heady feeling.

They stuck to innocuous topics during dinner. Austin had changed out of his work gear into a sport coat and dark slacks. His white shirt and blue tie showed off his tan.

The man was too handsome for his own good.

Despite her best efforts, Brooke couldn't keep herself from repeatedly sneaking a peek at that tiny, telltale white line on the third finger of Austin's left hand. She noticed it every time he reached for the bread basket or picked up the saltshaker.

"I should tell you something," she said, the words threatening to stick in her throat.

Austin stilled, perhaps alerted by the note of gravity in her voice. "Oh?"

"My father stood up to my mother. It was remarkable, really. He said he would fund my art studio despite her wishes."

"What are you telling me, Brooke?"

Now she felt like a bug on the end of a pin. Austin's piercing gaze dissected her and found her wanting. "Just that my dreams are within reach with or without a marriage license."

That was a lie. A whopper, really. Her dreams were no longer limited to an empty, weed-choked lot in downtown Royal. Now they included a cowboy architect with a big smile and a closed-off heart.

The man in question picked up a silver iced teaspoon and rolled it between his long fingers. The repetitive motion mesmerized her.

"I thought we had a deal, Brooke. You've bought a dress. I've ordered flowers. The appointment with the judge is on the books."

She reached across the table and took the spoon out of his hand. Then she linked his fingers with hers, feeling his warm, comforting grasp ground her…give her courage. "I know what we said. But I want you to know there's an escape clause. You can bail right now. Free and clear."

Part of her wanted him to take the bait. So that she would no longer be clinging to this terrible, fruitless yearning to lay claim to this man's heart and soul.

Austin squeezed her fingers. His smile was both sweet and mockingly erotic. "I know what I want, Brooke. You're the only one dithering."

And there it was. The challenge.

She took a deep breath. "Okay, then. If you're sure. I asked Alexis about Wednesday morning. She's free."

"Good."

He reached into his pocket and extracted a slim white envelope. "This is for you, Brooke."

She took it from him gingerly. "What is it?"

"Open it, honey. You'll see."

Inside was a gift certificate to a baby store in Dallas. The certificate had a lot of zeroes at the end. "Austin," she said softly. "This is too much."

"Get everything you need for the nursery. Everything. You can wait until we know if it's a boy or a girl, or you can go with a unisex theme and start shopping now. I want you to have plenty of time to get the baby's room ready. If you'd like to paint, I can handle that on the weekends."

"I don't know what to say."

He rubbed the back of her hand with his thumb, sending tingles down her spine. "Tell me you're happy, Brooke."

That was a heck of an order. Why did he have to ask for so much?

"I'm happy," she whispered, her throat tight. "Of course I'm happy."

It was clear from his face that her words were not entirely convincing.

Even so, he smiled. "Ready to get settled into our new digs?"

"Oh, yes. I forgot we'll have to make up beds."

"Nope. I had a service come in today. They've outfitted the entire house with the basics, so we'll be all set until we have time to pick out our own things. And they've stocked the fridge and cabinets with staples and perishable items."

"Looks like you've thought of everything."

"I tried," he said. "We'll see how well I did."

Fifteen

Austin kept waiting for the other shoe to drop. Brooke seemed matter-of-fact about their new living arrangements, but he couldn't be sure what she was thinking. The woman had learned to hide her emotions and feelings from him. He didn't like the change. Not one bit.

On a more positive note, she was less frazzled now. Clearly she had come to terms with her pregnancy. He could almost see the mental switch that had flipped inside her. Deciding to embrace motherhood wholeheartedly was a huge step.

At the condo, she flitted from room to room, examining every nook and cranny, though she had seen it all twice before. He gave her space. She was nervous. Understandably so.

For his part, Austin was glad not to be living in the

bunkhouse at the Lone Wolf anymore. He had appreciated Gus's hospitality, but it was time to put down more
permanent roots, at least for the short term. The irony
of that equivocation didn't escape him.

As the hour grew later, Brooke got quieter. It occurred to him that she was on edge about the sleeping
arrangements. That was easy enough to fix. He didn't
want her coming to him out of any sense of obligation.

When they passed in the hall for the fifth or sixth
time, he put out a hand and caught her by the wrist. Her
bones felt small and fragile in his grasp. "Relax, honey.
You have your own room."

She chewed her lower lip, making no pretense of
misunderstanding. "I know. But I thought we agreed
this would be a real marriage."

Her anxiety caught him off guard. And though he
would be loath to admit such a thing, it hurt. "I'm not
buying a wife," he said, the words sharper than he had
intended.

She flinched. "I didn't mean it like that."

"Look," he said. He stopped, scraped his fingers
through his hair and pressed the heel of his hand to his
forehead. He sighed. "I need to go to Dallas tomorrow.
Just for the day. Why don't you come with me?"

"No," she said quickly. "There's lots to do here." She
grimaced. "Do you have to go?"

He shrugged. "Jenny's father died this past week-
end. They've asked me to say a word at the funeral. I
don't want to. Not really. But I couldn't think of a polite way to say no."

"I'm so sorry." Brooke's expression was stricken.

"We should postpone the wedding. You'll be expected to stay longer than one day, surely."

"Brooke…"

She stood there staring at him. "What?"

"This isn't because of Jenny. It's not, I swear. I'm not doing this for her. But her mom…well, she…"

"She loves you," Brooke said, her voice flat.

"Yes. I know it's been a long time. It shouldn't matter."

"People are entitled to their feelings, Austin. I understand that. You should be honored."

"I wanted this to be a special week for you and me."

She wrapped her arms around her waist. "I'm not a child. Things happen. Please don't worry about me. Do what you have to do."

Austin went to bed alone that night. He lay in the darkness on an unfamiliar mattress with his hands linked behind his head and tried not to think about Brooke sleeping just a few feet down the hall.

His sex hardened as he imagined her soft body tucked up against his. The scent of her hair was familiar to him now. The curve of her bottom. The way her breasts warmed in his palms.

In less than forty-eight hours, she would be his wife. At one time, that notion would have scared him. Now he was confident he could handle it. Brooke knew the score. She understood what he could give and what he couldn't.

Despite his very real aversion to opening himself up to an intimate relationship, this was going to be a good thing.

He was looking forward to fatherhood. Brooke was going to be an amazing mom, even though she was understandably scared. Hell, so was he. What did he know about raising a kid? But it was something he wanted, something he had always wanted.

Jenny's death had been the death of that dream, too.

In the silence of the darkened room, he could hear himself breathing. Soon, Brooke would be here beside him. He couldn't deny the rush of pleasure and anticipation in his gut at that thought.

Brooke was awakening feelings in him that he'd been sure he would never experience again. Affection. Warmth. The need to protect.

To say that he was conflicted was like saying Texas was a big state. He was looking forward to his new future. But at the same time, he was skittish.

He didn't want to hurt Brooke. But his heart wasn't up for grabs. Period.

Though it pissed him off, Brooke managed to avoid him the following morning. He was forced to head for the airport without seeing her at all. Leaving town with things rocky between them made him uneasy.

They were supposed to be getting married tomorrow, so why was that prospect seeming less and less likely?

The funeral was difficult and sad. Seeing Jenny's mother even more so. He had dreaded coming, because he thought it would cause him to relive every minute of Jenny's funeral. In the end, that didn't happen. Not really.

His grief was different now. It would always be a

part of his past, but it was no longer a searing pain that controlled his days.

The realization brought first dumb shock, then quiet gratitude.

At last the funeral and the accompanying social niceties were over. Traffic on the way back to the airport made him miss his flight. He cooled his heels for an hour and a half and finally caught a later flight. After a hot, crowded hop to Royal, he landed and retrieved his truck for the drive to his new home.

The condo was dark when he arrived. It was after eleven. It made sense that Brooke would be asleep.

Disappointment flooded his stomach as he unlocked the front door and let himself in quietly. He stood in the foyer and listened. Not a sound broke the silence.

With a sigh, he carried his bag to his bedroom and tossed it on the chair beside the bed. After a long, hot shower, he felt marginally more human.

His lonely bed held no attraction at all. Wearing nothing but a pair of clean boxers, he tiptoed down the hall and stopped at Brooke's door. It was not closed completely. He eased it open and stood in the doorway until his eyes grew accustomed to the semidark. Her body was a small lump under the covers. A dim nightlight cast illumination from the bathroom.

This entire day he had been driven by a need to return home. Here. To this house. A place where he had slept only one night so far and that could not—by any conceivable standard—possibly be considered home already.

What had drawn him back from Dallas was more

than drywall and shingles and wooden studs. The invisible homing beacon was wrapped up in a petite woman with a big heart and an endless capacity for hope.

Guilt flooded him without warning, leaving sickness in its wake. He was about to marry her tomorrow for no other reason than because she drove the cold away. And he needed that. He needed her.

But it wasn't love. It couldn't be. Never again.

He couldn't even pretend to himself that he was her savior. Brooke's father had offered to finance her studio dream. Brooke didn't need Austin at all anymore. The best he could offer was giving the baby his name.

He must have inadvertently made a sound. The lump beneath the covers moved. Brooke sat up in bed, scrubbing her face like a child. "Austin? Sorry. I was waiting up for you. I must have dozed off."

Her hair was loose around her shoulders. The scent of her shampoo reached him where he stood. She was wearing an ivory camisole that clung to her small breasts.

"I didn't mean to wake you."

"It's okay. How was the funeral?"

He shrugged, one hand clenched on the door frame to keep himself in check. "It was fine. Saw a lot of old friends."

"And your mother-in-law?"

"She'll be okay, I think. Her sister is going to move in with her. She's a widow, too."

The silence built for a few seconds.

Then Brooke held out a hand. "You must be exhausted. And cold. Come get in bed with me."

He stumbled toward the promise of salvation, knowing full well that he was a selfish bastard who would take and take and give nothing in return.

Brooke lifted the covers and squeaked when he climbed in. "Your feet are like ice," she said.

"Sorry." He spooned her from behind, dragging her close and wrapping his arms around her so tightly she protested. His world was spinning. Brooke was his anchor. He rested his cheek on the smooth plane of her back. "Go to sleep, honey. It's after midnight."

"But you're…"

He had an erection. Pike hard. Impossible to hide.

"Doesn't matter," he said.

For hours he drifted in and out of sleep. It was as if he was afraid to let down his guard. He'd been half convinced she would bolt when he was out of town. Until he had his ring on her finger, he couldn't be sure this peace would last.

Exhaustion finally claimed him. When he next awoke in the faint gray light of dawn, Brooke had scooted on top of him and joined their bodies. She kissed him lazily, nipping his bottom lip and sucking it until he groaned aloud.

He was too aroused for gentleness. He gripped her ass and pulled her into him. Feeling her from this angle was sensory overload. He shoved up her camisole and toyed with her raspberry nipples.

Brooke's head fell back. She cried out. He felt the ripple of inner muscles caressing his hard length as she found her release.

Groaning and cursing, he rolled them in a tumble of

covers. Lifting her leg onto his shoulder, he went deeper still, thrusting all the way to the mouth of her womb, claiming her, marking her, saying with his body what the words would never offer. She was his.

They slept again.

The next time they surfaced, pale sunshine spilled into the room.

Brooke stirred drowsily, yawning and stretching like a little cat. She burrowed her face into his side. "Don't wanna get up," she mumbled.

He tightened an arm around her and kissed the top of her head, feeling a bone-deep contentment inexplicably overlaid with dread. "It's your wedding day, sweetheart."

She opened one eyelid. "Don't you mean *our* wedding day?"

His face heated. "Yes. Of course." Pressure built in his chest. He wanted to *do* something, *say* something.

But he couldn't.

Instead, he nuzzled her cheek with his and climbed out from under the covers. It was an asinine thing to do. Any man with an ounce of testosterone would have stayed right there and claimed what was his.

But a chasm had opened at his feet. Terrifying. Endlessly deep.

He'd been down that canyon once before.

"How long before you'll be ready to leave?" he asked, feigning cheerfulness.

Brooke rolled to her back, her expression hard to read, though she seemed more resigned than delighted about her upcoming nuptials. "Half an hour, I guess."

"Sounds good."

He shaved and dressed with little recollection of his jerky, automatic movements. Putting on his newest suit with a crisp white shirt and a royal blue tie made him marginally calmer.

He'd worn a tux when he married Jenny. This was not the same at all.

The florist delivered Brooke's bouquet right on time. Austin signed for it and tipped the guy.

In the meantime, he texted back and forth with Audra. She was meeting them in Joplin. At her insistence, she had procured a small cake for afterward at her house.

Austin was completely unprepared when Brooke walked out of the bedroom. The sight of her as a bride, even a less than formal one, slammed into his chest like a gunshot. And was equally painful.

Her blond hair was caught up on top of her head in one of those fancy knots women manage, with little wisps artfully framing her flushed cheeks. Subtle makeup emphasized smoky gray eyes. Soft lips covered in pale raspberry gloss made him want to snatch her up before any other man caught a glimpse of her delicate beauty.

The dress she had chosen was perfection. Her shoulders were bare. Ivory silk flattered her delicate curves. The skirt was narrow with a hint of swish. Her legs, those legs that could twine around his back and take him to heaven, looked a million miles long. Ivory pumps to match her dress had three-inch stiletto heels that gave her more height than usual.

He tried to swallow the boulder in his throat. "You look breathtaking."

Her smile was more cautious than radiant. "At least the dress still fits. I suppose that's the upside of being sick every morning."

"Is it awful? Even now?"

She lifted one pale, perfect shoulder. "I think we may be getting past the worst of it. We'll see."

"Good."

He hated the stilted conversation, hated the distance she had set between them.

He knew why the awkward wall was there. Brooke was protecting herself. Austin had insisted on a sterile, emotionless union, so his bride was doing her best not to *care*.

His own jacked-up psyche had created this mess.

Brooke reached for her clutch purse. "We should go. Alexis will be waiting."

Alexis had offered to meet them in Joplin, but Brooke had insisted her friend travel with them. Austin wasn't an idiot. His bride didn't want an intimate car ride with him.

Outside on the front porch, they both huddled into their coats. If the weather was any harbinger of marital luck, they were doomed. November had come in with steel-gray skies and chilling rain.

Austin struggled to lock the front door. The new key wanted to stick. "Damn it," he said, after it got stuck a third time and he had to take it out and try again.

Brooke hopped from one foot to the other. "I'm going to wait in the truck. I'm freezing."

"Wait," he said. "You'll ruin your dress. Let me hold the umbrella."

At the last moment, the dead bolt finally clunked as it was supposed to. He dropped the keys in his jacket pocket and reached for the large black umbrella. But Brooke had already taken it and stepped off the porch.

In slow motion, her shoe hit the top step—the newly painted top step that was slick as glass in the pouring rain. Her flimsy heels wobbled, giving no purchase as all. As he watched in horror, unable to reach her, she fell down seven stairs, striking her shoulder and her head and finally crumpling onto the sidewalk.

His entire body was paralyzed. A roaring in his head made it almost impossible to think. To breathe.

He was at her side in seconds, calling 9-1-1. Feeling like a fool because he couldn't remember his new address.

"Brooke. Brooke, sweetheart."

Her eyes were closed. A large, ugly bruise already bloomed on her right cheekbone. Blood seeped from a gash just above it. He wanted to scoop her up and hold her, but he was terrified to risk further injuries.

He knew the first-aid drill. Brooke might have damaged her spine during the fall. To lift her limp body could do irreparable harm.

Shrugging out of his coat, he draped it over her, covering as much of her small, broken body as he could. He left her only long enough to retrieve the damned umbrella. Then he opened it and crouched beside her, keeping the rain at bay as best he could.

With one hand, he stroked her face, held her wrist,

felt her pulse. "Hang on, Brooke. Help is on the way. You're going to be fine." Though it seemed her heart beat strongly, what did he know?

Royal's emergency services were top-notch. Austin knew they must have arrived in mere minutes. But the delay seemed like an eternity.

When at last they pulled up with a cacophony of sirens and a barrage of flashing lights, he should have felt relief. Instead, he was numb. The fear had overtaken him…had frozen every cell in his body.

Forced to step back, he watched, agonized, as they eased Brooke onto a board and strapped her down. Started an IV. Wrapped her in a blanket.

"She's pregnant," he blurted out suddenly. "She's pregnant."

One of the female EMTs gave him a sympathetic smile. "We'll take good care of her, sir. You can meet us at the hospital. Okay?"

He nodded. Hospital. Right. Not a courthouse. Not today.

He should call Audra. And Alexis.

The idea of making meaningful conversation was beyond him.

Instead, he took Brooke's phone from her purse and found Alexis's info. Adding Audra's number to the text, he sent word to both of them.

Brooke fell. We're at the hospital. I don't know about the baby.

His own cell phone rang immediately. He didn't answer. He couldn't speak. He was so cold and so scared and so damned helpless.

He couldn't lose someone again. He couldn't.

In retrospect, he shouldn't have driven himself to the hospital. There was no time to waste, though, so he did it anyway.

The emergency room waiting area was crowded. After struggling to find a parking space, he was then forced to cool his heels for several minutes before it was finally his turn at the counter.

"They brought my fiancée in by ambulance," he said. "Brooke Goodman?"

The woman consulted her computer. "The triage nurses are with her now. As soon as they get her in a cubicle, I can send you back."

"Can you tell me anything?"

The middle-aged woman, harried, impersonal, glanced at him a second time, and whatever she saw on his face must have cut through her professional reserve, because her expression softened. "I'm sorry. I can't give out any information like that. But it won't be long. Please take a seat, and I'll call you."

Sixteen

Brooke stirred, tried to breathe and groaned as a sharp pain lanced through her chest. A feminine voice broke through the fog. "Easy, Brookie. Not so fast. I'll hold a straw to your mouth. Open your lips."

It was simpler to cooperate than to protest. A trickle of cool liquid soothed her parched throat.

Why was she here? What happened to her?

Moments later, she sank back into sleep.

Her dreams were not pleasant. In them, she struggled. She cried out. And always, the pain.

Gradually, the fog receded. But the pain did not. Breathing was agony. "Alexis?" Her voice sounded thin and reedy.

"I'm here, baby. What do you need?"

"More water, please."

Swallowing didn't hurt. As long as she stayed perfectly still.

Unfortunately, that wasn't going to be an option for much longer. An overly cheerful nurse came in and unhooked an IV. "Gotta get this young lady up and moving around before pneumonia sets in. I'll be back shortly."

Brooke put an arm over her face. "Damn, that hurts."

Alexis pulled a chair closer to the bed. "You have two cracked ribs. And a broken wrist. The wrist required surgery. But everything is going to heal nicely. Those ribs will give you hell, though. Nothing they can do about that."

Gradually, snippets began to return. Her wedding day. The rainy morning. A slow-motion tumble off the porch. She remembered hearing Austin's panicked shout. Her own scream. And then multiple jolts of pain before she blacked out.

"The baby?" she croaked, suddenly terrified. "What about the baby?"

Alexis stroked her hand. "The doctor says the baby is fine. There was a bit of bleeding initially. They were concerned you might lose the pregnancy, but that has settled down. Your poor body took the brunt of the damage. They can't give you the best pain meds, though, because of the pregnancy. That's why you're hurting."

"Ah…"

Brooke turned her head slowly and scanned the room. As far as she could tell, she was in one of the very luxurious private suites at Royal Memorial Hospital.

Alexis hovered. "Can I get you anything?"

"What day is it?"

"Thursday afternoon. They'll bring you dinner shortly. You didn't get to eat yesterday because of the surgery. Then today when you woke up, the morning sickness kicked in. They're concerned about your weight."

"Where's Austin?" She couldn't hold back the words any longer.

Alexis blanched. "Well, um…"

The door opened and a familiar redhead walked into the room. She smiled gently at Brooke. "We've met. I'm Audra."

"Austin's sister."

"Yes."

"Where is he?"

The other two women looked at each other and back at Brooke. Alexis swallowed. "We're not exactly sure, honey. He took off."

Brook tried to sit up in the bed, alarmed. "What do you mean?" Pain forced her back down.

Audra took over the narrative. "Austin was here with you when Alexis and I arrived. He stayed through the surgery, until the doctor assured all of us you were safe and out of the woods. And then he…"

"Then he left." Alexis had a militant look in her eyes. "No one knows where he is. I'm sorry, Brooke."

Before Brooke could process that extraordinary information, the officious nurse was back. With the help of Audra and Alexis, the uniformed professional hustled Brooke out of bed and into a robe before making her stand and take a stroll down the corridor and back.

At first the pain was enough to make Brooke's forehead bead with sweat. Gradually, it subsided to a dull ache. Her legs moved slowly, as if she had been bedridden for a week and not a mere thirty-six hours.

Finally, the ordeal was over and she was allowed to return to her bed.

She fell asleep almost instantly.

When she awoke, Brooke instinctively looked for Austin, but her heart cried out in disbelief. He was nowhere in sight. Only Audra was in the room.

Austin's sister was as gentle as Alexis and even more comfortable with the routine. Brooke remembered that she had been—or still was—a nurse. "Thank you for helping me," Brooke said. She didn't know the protocol for dealing with Austin's sister.

All she could think about was Austin admitting that Audra had said marrying Brooke was a bad idea.

Great. Just great.

The dinner trays were delivered. As darkness fell outside the window, Brooke made herself eat.

Audra didn't say much.

When Brooke had finished half a baked chicken breast and some mashed potatoes, Audra sighed. "My brother isn't answering his cell phone. But while you were sleeping, this was delivered by hand to the front desk."

It was a plain white envelope with the word *Brooke* scribbled on the front. Though Brooke had never actually seen Austin's handwriting, the bold masculine scrawl was somehow familiar.

Her hands shook as she opened it.

Dear Brooke,

I've moved my things out of the condo for the moment. I want you to be comfortable there. And I'm trying to clear my head. If you need anything at all, Audra has access to my accounts. I'll be in touch soon.

AB

Brooke handed the single sheet of paper to Austin's sister. "I don't really know what this means." Horrible feelings assaulted her. Hurt. Abandonment. A deep sense of betrayal.

Audra glanced at the terse note and winced. "Nor do I. But he was a mess yesterday. Don't give up on him, Brooke. Please. I love my brother, and I want him to be happy."

Brooke's throat hurt. Some aspects about this interlude were going to take far longer to heal than a broken wrist. "The songwriters and poets tell us we each have one great love in our lives."

"That's bull crap. Austin loved Jenny. Of course he did. But I've seen a change in him since he met you. I have to believe that means something."

"Wishing doesn't make it so." The facts were damning.

Both Austin and Brooke had struggled with mixed emotions about marrying for the baby's sake. Austin had been willing to help Brooke secure her inheritance, but once her father relented, that excuse was no longer valid.

In the end, the wedding hadn't happened. Now, it

likely never would. Even though she knew it was probably for the best, the crushing weight in her chest made it hard to breathe.

The following morning Brooke convinced Alexis to take her home—to the condo, though Brooke's friend was not at all happy about it. "Come to my house, damn it," Alexis said. "We have a million servants. You'll recover in the lap of luxury. I don't want you spending time alone."

Actually, time alone sounded heavenly. Brooke needed to be on her own to lick her wounds and regroup. "I'll be fine," she insisted. "The doctor said I don't have any special restrictions. They gave me plastic to wrap around the cast when I shower, and the ribs themselves will be self-limiting. I have to move slowly or pay the price."

"You are *so* stubborn."

Brooke grinned. "Pot. Kettle." She slipped her arms into the loose cardigan Alexis had brought to the hospital. That, along with a solid T-shirt and knit stretchy pants were destined to be Brooke's wardrobe for the near future.

At the moment, she and Alexis were waiting on the nurse to bring the discharge forms.

Audra had driven back to Joplin late last night.

Austin had been spotted on the job site at the club this morning, but that was the only information Brooke had been able to pry out of her closemouthed friend.

Brooke picked at a loose thread on her sweater. "Where's my wedding dress? Is it ruined?"

Alexis grimaced. "I won't lie. It was a mess. Blood. Mud. A rip or two. But my dry cleaner is a miracle worker. I took it to him yesterday and promised him a pair of tickets to the charity gala if he could work his magic."

"You didn't have to do that."

"For you, Brookie, anything." Alexis paced the confines of the small room. "You won't be able to work at the club for a few weeks, but not to worry. I'll pay you anyway. You know…sick leave."

"Don't be absurd. I'm on contract. Sick leave wasn't part of our agreement."

Alexis bristled, her eyes flashing. At times like this, Brooke could see the resemblance to her grandfather. "It's *my* budget and *my* event. I can do as I please."

Brooke blinked back tears. She was dispirited and exhausted and barely hanging on to hope for the future. In spite of everything, she missed Austin's steady, comforting presence, his support. And she missed *him*. He was like a drug her body craved without ceasing.

To have Alexis in her corner meant everything. "Thank you. At least it was my left hand. I can still work on pencil sketches for the day-care murals. So I won't fall completely behind."

"Well, there you go."

Soon, the paperwork was complete, and they were on their way.

The most logical route from the hospital to the condo would have taken them directly past the Cattleman's Club. Instead, Alexis drove three blocks out of the way.

Brooke pretended not to notice.

When they reached the street where Austin had leased a home for himself and his child and his temporary wife, Brooke struggled with a great wave of sadness. She had tried so hard to do the right things in her life.

Yet lately, everything she touched seemed to turn to ashes.

The attached garage at the back of the house made it possible for Brooke to enter the condo by negotiating only two steps. If she and Austin had gone out this way on Wednesday, the accident never would have happened. She would be his wife by now.

A shiver snaked its way down her spine, though the day was warm. In true Royal fashion, the cold snap had moved on. Now November was showing her balmy side. Who knew how long it would last? And who knew if Brooke would ever again share Austin's bed?

Alexis helped her inside and went back to unload Brooke's few personal possessions from the car. In the meantime, Brooke stood in the doorway of Austin's bedroom and surveyed the emptiness. He hadn't been kidding. Every trace of his presence had been erased from the condo.

Was he avoiding *her*? Or a ghost who wouldn't let go?

Alexis made a pass through the kitchen, muttering to herself. "You have the basics," she said. "But I'll send over meals, at least for a few days. The doctor says you're to do nothing but rest and get light exercise."

"Yes, ma'am." Brooke smiled. "I would hug you, but I don't think I can."

Alexis smirked. "I'll take a rain check. Seriously, Brookie. Promise me you'll text any time, night or day. I won't sleep a wink worrying about you."

"I swear. I'll be a model patient."

"Okay. I've got to get to the club. I'll send over lunch, and I'll check on you midafternoon."

The day dragged by. Brooke had never been much of a TV fan. She wasn't in the mood for a movie, either.

Instead, she listened to music, talked to the baby, worked on her sketches and pondered her immediate life choices. The past three months had changed her. She was done letting other people control her fate. She and her child were a unit. A family. It was up to Brooke to create a home and a future for her son or daughter.

Saturday ambled along as slowly as the day before. Some tiny part of her hoped to see Austin, but it was a futile wish. He had missed a day of work for his father-in-law's funeral and another day of work for the almost wedding and the hospital kerfuffle. He would need today to catch up, especially in light of the glorious weather.

By the time Sunday rolled around, Brooke was feeling much better physically. The jagged fissure in her heart was another matter. Every time she walked past Austin's door, the empty room mocked her.

For all her brave notions of independence, she hadn't quite figured out her next step when it came to housing. Should she stay? Should she go? Would Austin ever want to come back to the condo?

With every hour that passed, more questions arose. Around three in the afternoon, the sunshine was so bright and so beautiful, she couldn't resist any longer. Grabbing a blanket from the closet, she made her way to the small, private backyard, spread her cover on the ground and stretched out on her back.

Getting down was harder than she'd anticipated. Her damaged ribs protested vociferously. But once she was settled, she closed her eyes and sighed. She had slathered her face and arms with sunscreen, so she had no qualms about soaking up the warm rays.

With her hands tucked behind her head and her legs crossed at the ankles, she concentrated on relaxing her entire body, muscle by muscle. Peace came slowly but surely.

No one had ever died from a broken heart.

Loving Austin was a gift. A bright, wonderful gift. As much as it hurt to contemplate letting him go, knowing him had brought her immeasurable joy.

Still, knowing that didn't stop the flood of aching regret and the stab of agony over everything she had lost.

When she awoke, the angle of the sun told her she had slept for a long time. It was no wonder. Her body was still playing catch-up.

Instead of rolling to her feet—a move that would most certainly involve a sharp jolt of pain—she stayed very still and amused herself by cataloging the myriad sounds in her new neighborhood.

Despite the calendar, someone nearby was mowing their lawn. Dogs, more than one, barked. Staking a claim. Marking territory.

Childish laughter was harder to catch in the distance, but it was there.

As she wrinkled her brow and concentrated on the odd plinking sound nearby, a shadow fell across her body.

She shielded her eyes. "Alexis?" No one else had a key.

No one but Austin.

He crouched beside her. "No. It's me."

If she tried to sit up, it would hurt. He would try to help, and he would touch her, and she would fall apart.

So she didn't move. "What are you doing here?"

"I live here," he said.

"Do you? I wasn't sure."

"You're angry," he said.

"No. Not angry. Confused maybe. And sad." She shielded her eyes. The sun was low on the horizon. "What time is it?"

"Almost five."

"No wonder I'm hungry."

She tried to speak matter-of-factly, but her heart was racing. No matter his reasons for coming, this conversation was going to be tough.

Austin sat down on his butt, propped up one knee and slung an arm over it. "Aren't you cold?"

"I wasn't earlier. I guess it's cooling off now."

"Can I help you up?"

She shook her head. "I can do it myself. Please don't touch me."

He flinched. Perhaps the words had come out too

harshly. That wasn't her problem. She was in self-preservation mode.

Taking a deep breath, she rolled to her side, scrambled to her knees and cursed as pain grabbed her middle and squeezed. Then at last, she was on her feet. "We should go inside," she said. "It's going to get dark."

Without waiting to see if he would follow her, she clung to the stair rail and hobbled up the steps one at a time, as if she were an old lady.

Inside the house, she made her way to the den. One of the recliners had become her nest of choice. It was relatively easy to get in and out of, and once she was settled, it didn't put pressure on her ribs.

She stood behind the chair, using it as a shield. "Is this going to take long?"

"Stop doing that," he said, the words laced with irritation.

"Doing what?"

"Acting weird."

Her eyebrows shot to her hairline. "*I'm* acting weird? Give me a break, Austin. I'm not the one who disappeared into thin air."

She tried to study him dispassionately, as a stranger would. His face was haggard, as if he had aged ten years in a handful of days. He looked thinner. Paler. There was an air of suffering about him.

He was wearing an ancient leather aviator's jacket and jeans. The soft, long-sleeved Henley shirt underneath was a caramel color that complemented his dark brown eyes.

Everything about him was intensely masculine. The

casual clothes, slightly unkempt blond hair and ruggedly handsome stance made him the poster boy for *lone wolf*. Brooke got the message loud and clear.

She was trembling inside, but she dared not let it show. Not for anything in the world would she let him think his desertion had crippled her. She could stand on her own.

She *would* stand on her own. She had no other choice.

Seventeen

Austin wasn't sure what he had been expecting, but it wasn't this. Brooke looked at him as if they were strangers. She didn't appear to be angry. If anything, all of her usual animation had been erased.

He was accustomed to her laughter and her quick wit and her zest for life. This woman was a shadow.

"How are you feeling?" he asked gruffly. It had infuriated him to find out that Brooke was alone...that neither Alexis nor Audra was by her side.

"I'm fine," Brooke said. "Sore, of course, but that will pass. This little cast isn't too much of a bother since it's on my left wrist. I won't have to wear it very long."

"And the baby?"

"One hundred percent perfect."

"Good."

His chest ached. His throat hurt. His head throbbed.

Brooke was so beautiful, he wanted to grab her up and hold her until the terrible ice inside him melted. But the fear was greater than the wanting.

She bit her bottom lip, a sure sign she was nervous or upset or both. "Where do we go from here, Austin?"

He hadn't expected the blunt question.

"Stay as long as you like," he muttered.

"So you're going to support the baby and me out of the goodness of your heart?"

The snippy sarcasm raked his raw mood. "I'm trying to be the good guy in this situation."

"News flash. You failed."

He reared back, affronted. "What do you want from me, damn it?"

"An explanation would be nice. I never tried to trap you into anything, Austin. I'm not sure why you felt the need to hide out."

"It's complicated."

"Try me." Brooke glared at him, her gray gaze stormy. Her cheekbones were too pronounced. Her turquoise knit top and cream sweater swallowed her small, delicate frame. Even though she wore thin black leggings, there was no visible sign of a baby bump yet.

"Do we have any coffee?" he asked.

Brooke frowned. "That's all you're going to say?"

He put a hand to the top of his head, where a jackhammer burrowed into his skull. "Let me have some caffeine," he pleaded. "And I'll make us a couple of sandwiches. After that, I'll answer all your questions."

It was a magnanimous offer and one he might later regret. But he needed sustenance.

He followed Brooke to the kitchen, careful to keep his distance. Despite her injured ribs, she moved gracefully, putting coffee on to brew, getting out cups and saucers, directing him to what he needed for cobbling together thick roast beef sandwiches with slices of freshly cut Swiss cheese.

At last, they sat down at the table together.

He fell on the sandwich with a groan of appreciation.

Brooke ate hers with more finesse, though she eyed him with a frown. "When was the last time you had a real meal?"

"I don't know," he said. "Breakfast with you Wednesday morning, maybe? I've had a few packs of peanut butter crackers along the way. It's been busy at the club. Haven't felt much like eating."

Without another word she stood and fixed him a second sandwich.

Three cups of coffee later, he felt marginally more human.

When the plates were empty, there was nothing left but the silence.

He stood and paced again.

Brooke remained seated. He had already noticed that standing and sitting aggravated her ribs. It was a wonder she hadn't punctured a lung when she fell.

Dizziness assailed him, and he sat down hard. The image of Brooke tumbling down those damn stairs was one he couldn't shake. It haunted his dreams.

Her expression softened, as if she could see his inner turmoil. "Talk to me, Austin."

He dropped his head in his hands and groaned. "I lied to you from the beginning," he said.

She blinked at him. "I don't understand."

"You made the assumption that I was still in love with Jenny. That fiction suited my purposes, so I let you believe it. Even though I knew the lie caused you pain. So there. Now you know what kind of man I am."

Brooke's bottom lip trembled. "The day I met you was the first time you had taken off your wedding ring."

"That much was true. But I continued wearing the ring as long as I did because it kept women like you from getting ideas."

"Oh."

"I loved Jenny. Of course I did. But that wasn't why I wore my wedding ring for six long years. I wasn't still wallowing in my grief or clinging to her memory, not by that point. All I wanted was to be left alone. The ring was a useful deterrent."

He laid out the facts baldly, painting himself in the worst possible light. Brooke needed to know the whole truth.

"But you had taken it off that night when I met you."

He nodded. "Audra wouldn't let up. She said I was turning into a soulless jackass, and she insisted I return to the land of the living."

"I see."

"I *knew* you thought I was still in love with Jenny, Brooke. And I let you believe it. Aren't you going to ask me why?"

Her eyes were huge, her face pale. "Why, Austin?"

He scraped his hands through his hair. "Because you scared me more than anything that had happened to me in forever. You gave me a glimpse of light and warmth and happiness, and I wanted it. God, Brooke, I wanted it."

"But…"

"I was terrified," he said simply. "I don't know if I can make you understand. I don't know if anyone can understand unless they go through it. Watching a loved one die like Jenny died is worse than being sick yourself. She waded through hell. The truth is, I would literally have cut off one of my limbs, Brooke, to have spared her even a day of the agony. But I couldn't. She had to walk that road alone, and the best I could do was walk beside her."

"Walking beside someone is a lot. It's *everything*."

"It didn't seem that way. I've never felt so helpless in my life. So when I met you with your sunshiny spirit and your sweet smile and your utter joy for life, I wanted to let you into my heart and into my soul, but I was too damned scared."

"Scared of what?" she asked softly.

"Scared to care. I never want to feel that pain again."

Her heart sank. "But then I got pregnant and you had to come up with plan B."

"Exactly. Even then, I hedged my bets. I told myself I could sleep with you and provide for the baby, but that was my line in the sand."

"Then why marry me?"

He jumped to his feet, pacing again. Restless. Overwhelmed with a million conflicting emotions. "I don't know."

Brooke stood up slowly, wincing. "I think you do know, Austin." Her smile was wistful. As if her endless fount of hope had dried up.

"I wanted our child to be legitimate," he said.

"No one cares about that kind of thing anymore."

"They do in Royal."

"Maybe. But that's not why you agreed to my proposal, is it?"

"It was one reason." The other reason was harder to admit. Almost impossible, in fact.

He shoved his hands in his pockets to keep from reaching for her. "Are you sure the baby is okay?"

"Yes. Quit changing the subject." Brooke leaned back against the fridge, gingerly shifting her weight from one foot to the other. "Tell me how it felt when you saw me fall."

He gaped at her. *No!* Reliving that moment made him light-headed. "I was worried," he said. "It all happened so fast. I was afraid you were seriously injured. That you might never wake up. That you could have a miscarriage."

Big gray eyes stared at him, eyes that seemed to see deep inside to every screwed-up corner of his psyche. "Did you blame yourself, Austin?"

He started to shake. Ah. There it was. The truth. Again, he saw her tumbling down those damn stairs. He should have been close, holding her arm. "You didn't wait for me," he croaked.

"Exactly. And Jenny was a grown woman who could

why. You never wanted to hear any news regarding what was happening in Catalina Cove."

No, she hadn't, but anything having to do with K-Gee wasn't just town news. Bryce should have known that. "I'm sorry to hear about his parents. I really am. I'm surprised he's on the zoning board."

For years the townsfolk of the cove had never recognized members of the Pointe-au-Chien Native American tribe who lived on the east side of the bayou. Except for when it was time to pay city taxes. With K-Gee on the zoning board that meant change was possible in Catalina Cove after all.

"I need to know what you want to do, Vash," Bryce said, interrupting her thoughts. "The Barnes Group is giving us twenty days to finalize the deal or they will withdraw their offer."

Vashti stood up to cross the kitchen floor and put her teacup in the kitchen sink. "Okay, I'll think about what you said. Ten million dollars is a lot of money."

"Yes, and just think what you could do with it."

Vashti was thinking and she loved all the possibilities. Although she loved her job, she could stop working and spend the rest of her life traveling to all those places her aunt always wanted to visit but hadn't, because of putting Shelby by the Sea first. Vashti wouldn't make the same mistake.

THE NEXT MORNING, for the first time in two years, Vashti woke up feeling like she was in control of her life and could finally see a light—a bright one at that—at the end of the road. Scott was out of her life, she had a great have made an appointment and gone to the doctor for her cough long before she actually did." She released a shuddering breath. "I'm sorry I scared you. Truly, I am. But you're not in control of the world, Austin. You never were."

"You were unconscious," he said, reliving that horrific moment four days ago when he had lost his shit completely. "It was raining and you were wearing that beautiful silky wedding dress, and all I could do was crouch over you and pray you didn't lose the baby."

"Losing the baby would have solved your problem."

Fury rose in him, choked him, sickened him. "By God, don't you say that. Don't you *dare* say that!"

She wrapped her arms around her slender waist, fearless and unflinchingly brave in the face of his wrath.

"Why not, Austin? It's true."

The chasm was there at his feet again. No matter how much he backpedaled, he couldn't escape it. Brooke kept pushing him and pushing him. As though she thought he was brave enough to jump across. He wasn't brave. He was blind with fear.

She held out her hand, her smile tremulous. "Tell me why you were so upset when I fell. Tell me why you weren't at the hospital when I woke up. Tell me why you rented this beautiful condo for us and then moved out so I'm forced to sleep here all alone at night. Tell me, Austin. Why?"

He couldn't say it. If he did, fate would smack him down again...would bring him to his knees and punish him for daring to believe he might find happiness one more time in his life.

But he owed Brooke something for what he had put her through. She at least deserved the truth. Even if Austin had not turned out to be the man she thought he was.

Before he could speak, Brooke came to him and laid her head on his shoulder. She slid her arms around his waist. "You've given me so much, Austin. I wanted to break free of my parents' influence and stand on my own two feet. You helped me get there. I'll always be grateful to you for supporting me."

"*You* did that," he said. "You're brave and determined and so strong." He held her tightly, but with infinite gentleness. Her warmth broke through the last of his painful walls. "I love you, Brooke Goodman," he whispered. "Body and soul. Jenny was my first love, the love of my youth. You're my forever love, the mother of my child, the woman who will, please God, grow old with me."

"I love you, too, stupid cowboy. Don't ever leave me again."

Her voice broke on the last word, and she cried. The tears were cathartic for both of them. They clung to each other—forever, it seemed.

At last, Brooke pulled back and looked up at him, her eyelashes damp and spiky, her eyes red rimmed. "I'm not jealous of Jenny. I'm really not. I'm glad she had you when it mattered most."

Austin shook his head slowly, rescuing one last teardrop with his fingertip. "You are an extraordinary woman. But hear this, my sweet. I'm going to spend the next fifty years making up for the fact that your family hasn't appreciated you. I'm going to shower you with love and affection, and it's entirely possible that I may spoil you rotten."

A tiny grin tipped the corners of Brooke's mouth. "Is that a threat or a promise?"

He sighed deeply, feeling contentment roll through him like a golden river. "Either works. How do you feel about an after-Christmas wedding? With all the trimmings. I'm not a fan of the way we were headed the first time."

Brooke pouted. "I don't want to wait that long to be your wife."

"I'm open to debate, but we're staring down the gun at this auction thing. I have promises to keep. More importantly, I've decided you and I are going to take a grand honeymoon. Like in the old days, when couples went to Europe for a month. I want to take you to all those art galleries before the baby comes. How does that sound?"

She beamed up at him. "I think it sounds amazing. But I'd still be willing to do a quickie courthouse ceremony."

"Nope. We're going the whole nine yards. An engagement ring, for starters. And a bridal gown that will be the envy of every woman in Royal. Empire waisted, of course," he said with a grin.

"I love it." Brooke tried to dance around the kitchen and had to stop and grab the counter when her ribs protested.

"Plus," he said, "I'd like for my bride to be able to take a deep breath without being in pain."

"Details, details." Brooke waved a dismissive hand, but she was pale beneath her excitement-flushed cheeks.

"Then it's settled." He took her in his arms and kissed her slowly, long and deep. Lust filtered through his body, overlaid with gratitude and tenderness. Brooke's lips clung to his, her ragged breaths matching his own.

He wanted her so badly, he trembled.

But her injury made his hunger for her problematic. He released her and brushed a strand of hair from her forehead. "I can't sweep you off your feet right now, can I?"

"Not unless you want me to pass out."

"Duly noted. How do you feel about really, really careful sex?"

"I thought you'd never ask."

Brooke climbed up onto the mattress and watched Austin undress. She would suffer a dozen broken ribs if this were the payoff. Hearing Austin say he loved her made up for endless days of heartache.

He ditched the last of his clothing and joined her. Brooke had done her own restrained striptease moments earlier, because Austin was afraid of hurting her.

Now here they were. Both of them bruised and broken in different ways.

She ran a hand down his warm, hair-dusted thigh. "Did I ever tell you that my grandmother was a twin?"

Austin raised one eyebrow as he coaxed her nipples into tightly furled buds with his thumbs. "You might have forgotten to mention that."

"How do you feel about multiple babies?"

He nibbled the side of her neck. His big body was a furnace. "I like making them. A lot. And though I prefer them to arrive one at a time, I'll keep an open mind."

He scooted lower in the bed and kissed her still-flat tummy. "You're going to be the most beautiful pregnant woman in Royal."

"You might be a tad prejudiced."

"Maybe." He kissed the inside of her thigh.

Her breath hitched. "When you finish Matt Galloway's house, will you design one for us? I thought we could start looking for land in the meantime. And don't get all prissy about my inheritance. We can split the price fifty-fifty if it makes you feel better."

His grin was brilliant. Carefree. It made her heart swell with happiness and pride. "I could live with that." He eased her onto her side and scooted in behind her, joining their bodies with one gentle push. "Is this hurting you?"

She gasped as he shifted and his firm length hit a sensitive spot in her sex. "Yes, Cowboy. But only in the best possible way."

He kissed the nape of her neck, his breath warm. "I adore you, Brooke."

Pleasure rolled through her body in a shimmering wave. "You're mine, Austin. Now and forever. Don't you forget it."

Then, with a gentle, thorough loving, he took them home…

* * * * *

Will Gus and Rose succeed in keeping their grandchildren apart? Will the bachelor auction go off without a hitch?

Find out in His Until Midnight *by Reese Ryan!*

*When shy beauty Tessa Noble gets a makeover and steps in for her brother at a bachelor auction, she doesn't expect her best friend, rancher Ryan Bateman, to outbid everyone. But Ryan's attempt to protect her ignites a desire that changes everything...
Don't miss a single installment of the six-book
Texas Cattleman's Club: Bachelor Auction
Will the scandal of the century lead to love for these rich ranchers?*

Runaway Temptation
by USA TODAY *bestselling author Maureen Child*

Most Eligible Texan
by USA TODAY *bestselling author Jules Bennett*

Million Dollar Baby
by USA TODAY *bestselling author Janice Maynard*

His Until Midnight *by Reese Ryan*

The Rancher's Bargain *by Joanne Rock*

Lone Star Reunion *by Joss Wood*

In her brand-new series, New York Times *bestselling author Brenda Jackson welcomes you to Catalina Cove, where even the biggest heartbreaks can be healed...*

Turn the page for a sneak peek at Love in Catalina Cove

CHAPTER ONE

New York City

VASHTI ALCINDOR SHOULD be celebrating. After all, the official letter she'd just read declared her divorce final, which meant her three-year marriage to Scott Zimmons was over. Definitely done with. As far as she was concerned the marriage had lasted two years too long. She wouldn't count that first year since she'd been too in love to dwell on Scott's imperfections. Truth be told there were many that she'd deliberately overlooked. She'd been so determined to have that happily-ever-after that she honestly believed she could put up with anything.

But reality soon crept into the world of make-believe, and she discovered she truly couldn't. Her husband was a compulsive liar who could look you right in the eyes and lie with a straight face. She didn't want to count the number of times she'd caught him in the act. When she couldn't take the deceptions any longer she had packed her things and left. When her aunt Shelby died five months later, Scott felt entitled to half of the inheritance Vashti received in the will.

It was then that Vashti had hired one of the best divorce attorneys in New York, and within six weeks his private investigator had uncovered Scott's scandalous activities. Namely, his past and present affair with his boss's wife. Vashti hadn't wasted any time making Scott aware that she was not only privy to this information, but had photographs and videos to prove it.

Knowing she wouldn't hesitate to expose him as the lowlife that he was, Scott had agreed to an uncontested divorce and walked away with nothing. The letter she'd just read was documented proof that he would do just about anything to hold on to his cushy Wall Street job.

Her cell phone ringing snagged her attention, the ringtone belonging to her childhood friend and present Realtor, Bryce Witherspoon. Vashti clicked on her phone as she sat down at her kitchen table with her evening cup of tea. "Hey, girl, I hope you're calling with good news."

Bryce chuckled. "I am. Someone from the Barnes Group from California was here today and—"

"California?"

"Yes. They're a group of developers that's been trying to acquire land in the cove for years. They made you an unbelievably fantastic offer for Shelby by the Sea."

Vashti let out a loud shout of joy. She couldn't believe she'd been lucky enough to get rid of both her ex-husband and her aunt's property in the same day.

"Don't get excited yet. We might have problems," Bryce said.

Vashti frowned. "What kind of problems?"

"The developers want to tear down your aunt's bed-and-breakfast and—"

"Tear it down?" Vashti felt a soft kick in her stomach. Selling her aunt's bed-and-breakfast was one thing, having it demolished was another. "Why would they want to tear it down?"

"They aren't interested in the building, Vash. They want the eighty-five acres it sits on. Who wouldn't with the Gulf of Mexico in its backyard? I told you it would be a quick sale."

Vashti had known someone would find Shelby by the Sea a lucrative investment but she'd hoped somehow the inn would survive. With repairs it could be good as new. "What do they want to build there instead?"

"A luxury tennis resort."

Vashti nodded. "How much are they offering?" she asked, taking a sip of her tea.

"Ten million."

Vashti nearly choked. "Ten million dollars? That's nearly double what I was asking for."

"Yes, but the developers are eyeing the land next to it, as well. I think they're hoping that one day Reid Lacroix will cave and sell his property. When he does, the developers will pounce on the opportunity to get their hands on it and build that golf resort they've been trying to put there for years. Getting your land will put their foot in the door, so to speak."

Vashti took another sip of her tea. "What other problems are there?"

"This one is big. Mayor Proctor got wind of their offer and figured you might sell. He's calling a meeting."

"A meeting?"

"Yes, of the Catalina Cove zoning board. Although they can't stop you from selling the inn, they plan to block the buyer from bringing a tennis resort in here. The city ordinance calls for the zoning board to approve all new construction. This won't be the first time developers wanted to come into the cove and build something the city planners reject. Remember years ago when that developer wanted to buy land on the east end to build that huge shopping mall? The zoning board stopped it. They're determined that nothing in Catalina Cove changes."

"Well, it should change." As far as Vashti was concerned it was time for Mayor Proctor to get voted out. He had been mayor for over thirty years. When Vashti had left Catalina Cove for college fourteen years ago, developers had been trying to buy up the land for a number of progressive projects. The people of Catalina Cove were the least open-minded group she knew.

Vashti loved living in New York City where things were constantly changing and people embraced those changes. At eighteen she had arrived in the city to attend New York University and remained after getting a job with a major hotel chain. She had worked her way up to her six-figure salary as a hotel executive. At thirty-two she considered it her dream job. That wasn't bad for someone who started out working the concierge desk.

"Unless the Barnes Group can build whatever they want without any restrictions, there won't be a deal for us."

Vashti didn't like the sound of that. Ten million was ten million no matter how you looked at it. "Although I wouldn't want them to tear down Shelby, I think my aunt would understand my decision to do what's best for me." And the way Vashti saw it, ten million dollars was definitely what would be best for her.

"Do you really think she would want you to tear down the inn? She loved that place."

Vashti knew more than anyone how much Shelby by the Sea had meant to her aunt. It had become her life. "Aunt Shelby knew there was no way I would ever move back to Catalina Cove after what happened. Mom and Dad even moved away. There's no connection for me to Catalina Cove."

"Hey, wait a minute, Vash. I'm still here."

Vashti smiled, remembering how her childhood friend had stuck with her through thick and thin. "Yes, you're still there, which makes me think you need your head examined for not moving away when you could have."

"I love Catalina Cove. It's my home and need I remind you that for eighteen years it was yours, too."

"Don't remind me."

"Look, I know why you feel that way, Vash, but are you going to let that one incident make you have ill feelings about the town forever?"

"It was more than an incident, Bryce, and you know it." For Vashti, having a baby out of wedlock at sixteen had been a lot more than an incident. For her it had been a life changer. She had discovered who her real friends were during that time. Even now she would occasionally wonder how different things might have been had her child lived instead of died at birth.

"Sorry, bad choice of words," Bryce said, with regret in her voice.

"No worries. That was sixteen years ago." No need to tell Bryce that on occasion she allowed her mind to wander to that period of her life and often grieved for the child she'd lost. She had wanted children and Scott had promised they would start a family one day. That had been another lie.

"Tell me what I need to do to beat the rezoning board on this, Bryce," Vashti said, her mind made up.

"Unfortunately, to have any substantial input, you need to meet with the board in person. I think it will be beneficial if the developers make an appearance, as well. According to their representative, they're willing to throw in a few perks that the cove might find advantageous."

"What kind of perks?"

"Free membership to the resort's clubhouse for the first year, as well as free tennis lessons for the kids for a limited time. It will also bring a new employer to town, which means new jobs. Maybe if they were to get support from the townsfolk, the board would be more willing to listen."

"What do you think are our chances?"

"To be honest, even with all that, it's a long shot. Reid Lacroix is on the board and he still detests change. He's still the wealthiest person in town, too, and has a lot of clout."

"Then why waste my and the potential buyer's time?"

"There's a slim chance time won't be wasted. K-Gee is on the zoning board and he always liked you in school. He's one of the few progressive members on the board and the youngest. Maybe he'll help sway the others."

Vashti smiled. Yes, K-Gee had liked her but he'd liked Bryce even more and they both knew it. His real name was Kaegan Chambray. He was part of the Pointe-au-Chien Native American tribe and his family's ties to the cove and surrounding bayou went back generations, before the first American settlers.

Although K-Gee was two years older than Vashti and Bryce, they'd hung together while growing up. When Vashti had returned to town after losing her baby, K-Gee would walk Vashti and Bryce home from school every day. Even though Bryce never said, Vashti suspected something happened between Bryce and K-Gee during the time Vashti was away at that unwed home in Arkansas.

"When did K-Gee move back to Catalina Cove, Bryce?"

"Almost two years ago to help out his mom and to take over his family's seafood supply business when his father died. His mother passed away last year. And before you ask why I didn't tell you, Vash, you know job, but more importantly, some developer group was interested in her inn.

Her inn.

It seemed odd to think of Shelby by the Sea as hers when it had belonged to her aunt for as long as she could remember. Definitely long before Vashti was born. Her parents' home had been a mile away, and growing up she had spent a lot of her time at Shelby; especially during her teen years when she worked as her aunt's personal assistant. That's when she'd fallen in love with the inn and had thought it was the best place in the world.

Until…

Vashti pushed the "until" from her mind, refusing to go there and hoping Bryce was wrong about her having to return to Catalina Cove to face off with the rezoning board. There had to be another way and she intended to find it. Barely eighteen, she had needed to escape the town that had always been her safe haven because it had become a living hell for her.

An hour later Vashti had showered, dressed and was walking out her door ready to start her day at the Grand Nunes Luxury Hotel in Manhattan. But not before stopping at her favorite café on the corner to grab a blueberry muffin and a cup of coffee. Catalina Cove was considered the blueberry capital in the country, and even she couldn't resist this small indulgence from her hometown. She would be the first to admit that although this blueberry muffin was delicious, it was not as good as the ones Bryce's mother made and sold at their family's restaurant.

With the bag containing her muffin in one hand and

her cup of coffee in the other, Vashti caught the elevator up to the hotel's executive floor. She couldn't wait to get to work.

She'd heard that the big man himself, Gideon Nunes, was in town and would be meeting with several top members of the managerial and executive team, which would include her.

It was a half hour before lunch when she received a call to come to Mr. Nunes's office. Ten minutes later she walked out of the CEO's office stunned, in a state of shock. According to Mr. Nunes, his five hotels in the States had been sold, including this one. He'd further stated that the new owner was bringing in his own people, which meant her services were no longer needed.

In other words, she'd been fired.

CHAPTER TWO

A week later

VASHTI GLANCED AROUND the Louis Armstrong New Orleans International Airport. Although she'd never returned to Catalina Cove, she'd flown into this airport many times to attend a hotel conference or convention, or just to get away. Even though Catalina Cove was only an hour's drive away, she'd never been tempted to take the road trip to revisit the parish where she'd been born.

Today, with no job and more time on her hands than she really needed or wanted, in addition to the fact that there was ten million dollars dangling in front of her face, she was returning to Catalina Cove to attend the zoning board meeting and plead her case, although the thought of doing so was a bitter pill to swallow. When she'd left the cove she'd felt she didn't owe the town or its judgmental people anything. Likewise, they didn't owe her a thing. Now fourteen years later she was back and, to her way of thinking, Catalina Cove did owe her something.

#2629 HIS UNTIL MIDNIGHT
Texas Cattleman's Club: Bachelor Auction • by Reese Ryan
When shy beauty Tessa Noble gets a makeover and steps in for her brother at a bachelor auction, she doesn't expect her best friend, rancher Ryan Bateman, to outbid *everyone*. But Ryan's attempt to protect her ignites a desire that changes everything...

#2630 THE RIVAL'S HEIR
Billionaires and Babies • by Joss Wood
World-renowned architect Judah Huntley thought his ex's legacy would be permanent trust issues, not a baby! But when rival architect Darby Brogan steps in to help—for the price of career advice—playing house becomes hotter than they imagined...

#2631 THE RANCHER'S SEDUCTION
Alaskan Oil Barons • by Catherine Mann
When former rodeo king Marshall is injured, he reluctantly accepts the help of a live-in housekeeper to prepare his ranch for a Christmas fund-raiser. But soon he's fighting his desire for this off-limits beauty, and wondering what secrets Tally is hiding...

#2632 A CHRISTMAS PROPOSITION
Dallas Billionaires Club • by Jessica Lemmon
Scandal! The mayor's sister is marrying his nemesis! Except it's just a rumor, and now the heiress needs a real husband, fast. Enter her brother's sexy best friend, security expert Emmett Keaton. It's the perfect convenient marriage...until they can't keep their hands to themselves!

#2633 BLAME IT ON CHRISTMAS
Southern Secrets • by Janice Maynard
When Mazie Tarleton was sixteen, J.B. Vaughan broke her heart. Now she has him right where she wants him. But when they're accidentally locked in together, the spark reignites. Will she execute the perfect payback, or will he make a second chance work?

#2634 NASHVILLE REBEL
Sons of Country • by Sheri WhiteFeather
Sophie Cardinale wants a baby. Best friend and country superstar Tommy Talbot offers to, well, *help* her out. But what was supposed to be an emotions-free, fun fling suddenly has a lot more strings attached than either of them expected!

SPECIAL EXCERPT FROM

*Scandal! The mayor's sister is marrying his nemesis!
Except it's just a rumor, and now the heiress needs
a real husband, fast. Enter her brother's sexy
best friend, security expert Emmett Keaton. It's the
perfect convenient marriage...until they can't keep
their hands to themselves!*

*Read on for a sneak peek of
A Christmas Proposition by Jessica Lemmon,
part of her Dallas Billionaires Club series!*

His eyes dipped briefly to her lips, igniting a sizzle in the air that
had no place being there after he'd shared the sad story of his past.
Even so, her answering reaction was to study his firm mouth in
contemplation. The barely there scruff lining his angled jaw. His
dominating presence made her feel fragile yet safe at the same time.

The urge to comfort him—to comfort herself—lingered. This
time she didn't deny it.

With her free hand she reached up and cupped the thick column
of his neck, tugging him down. He resisted, but only barely, stopping
short a brief distance from her mouth to mutter one word.

"Hey..."

She didn't know if he'd meant to follow it with "this is a bad
idea" or "we shouldn't get carried away," but she didn't wait to find
out.

Her lips touched his gently and his mouth answered by puckering
to return the kiss. Her eyes sank closed and his hand flinched against
her palm.

He tasted…amazing. Like spiced cider and a capable, strong, heartbroken man who kept his hurts hidden from the outside world.

Eyes closed, she gripped the back of his neck tighter, angling her head to get more of his mouth. And when he pulled his hand from hers to come to rest on her shoulder, she swore she might melt from lust from that casual touch. His tongue came out to play, tangling with hers in a sensual, forbidden dance.

She used that free hand to fist his undershirt, tugging it up and brushing against the plane of his firm abs, and Emmett's response was to lift the hem of her sweater, where his rough fingertips touched the exposed skin of her torso.

A tight, needy sound escaped her throat, and his lips abruptly stopped moving against hers.

He pulled back, blinking at her with lust-heavy lids. She touched her mouth and looked away, the heady spell broken.

She'd just kissed her brother's best friend—a man who until today she might have jokingly described as her mortal enemy.

Worse, Emmett had kissed her back.

It was okay for this to be pretend—for their wedding to be an arrangement—but there was nothing black-and-white between them any longer. There was real attraction—as volatile as a live wire and as dangerous as a downed electric pole.

Whatever line they'd drawn by agreeing to marry, she'd stepped way, way over it.

He sobered quickly, recovering faster than she did. When he spoke, he echoed the words in her mind.

"That was a mistake."

Don't miss what happens next!
A Christmas Proposition by Jessica Lemmon,
part of her Dallas Billionaires Club series!

Available December 2018 wherever
Harlequin® Desire books and ebooks are sold.

www.Harlequin.com

HDEXP1118

Love Harlequin romance?

DISCOVER.

Be the first to find out about promotions, news and exclusive content!

Facebook.com/HarlequinBooks

Twitter.com/HarlequinBooks

Instagram.com/HarlequinBooks

Pinterest.com/HarlequinBooks

ReaderService.com

EXPLORE.

Sign up for the Harlequin e-newsletter and download a free book from any series at **TryHarlequin.com.**

CONNECT.

Join our Harlequin community to share your thoughts and connect with other romance readers!
Facebook.com/groups/HarlequinConnection

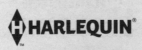

HARLEQUIN®

**ROMANCE WHEN
YOU NEED IT**

HSOCIAL2018

Reward the book lover in you!

Earn points on your purchase of new Harlequin books from participating retailers.

Turn your points into **FREE BOOKS** of your choice!

Join for FREE today at
www.HarlequinMyRewards.com.

Harlequin My Rewards is a free program (no fees) without any commitments or obligations.

MYR18